ETHICS MADE EASY

ETHICS MADE EASY

A NOVEL

001169|F

COLIN DOUGLAS

MAINSTREAM
PUBLISHING

ISBN 1 85158 014 X

Typeset in Garamond by Mainstream Publishing.
Printed by Billing & Sons, Ltd. Worcester.

Author's note

In real hospitals, there are strict rules governing experimentation upon patients; in fictional hospitals, of course, these rules may be partially or completely ignored.

Previous books in which Dr David Campbell has appeared are:
The Houseman's Tale,
The Greatest Breakthrough Since Lunchtime,
Bleeders Come First,
Wellies from the Queen,
A Cure for Living.
For Services to Medicine

The Houseman's Trilogy, is an omnibus edition including
The Houseman's Tale, The Greatest Breakthrough Since Lunchtime and
Bleeders Come First, which is now available from Mainstream Publishing.

I

In the thirty-eight minutes since Jean's phone call Campbell had finished an outpatient clinic and left the hospital; gone down to Marks and Spencers on Princes Street for bread, pâté, cheese, strawberries, white wine, Cinzano and lemonade; returned to his flat, set things out for lunch and changed the sheets and then, after some thought, taken the phone off the hook. He was ready. He took a last quick look round the flat then glanced at his watch again, just as the one o'clock gun went off.

'David . . . I'm really sorry.'

'It's all right.'

'It isn't. I'm ages late . . .' Jean stood close against Campbell, and he put his arms round her and kissed her brow. She nuzzled closer and her voice was muffled against his shoulder. 'Oh, I am sorry, David. Did you think I'd changed my mind?'

'No.'

'I tried to phone you . . . But you kept being engaged, so I thought . . . you'd given up on me and were ringing round trying to fix up a quick lunch with one of your other women.' Jean giggled but was vaguely upset as well, like someone turning up late for an urgent dental appointment.

He kissed her again. 'I took the phone off the hook so we wouldn't be disturbed.'

'By all your other women . . .' She laughed and hugged him. 'I'm really sorry I'm late. And it was for a silly reason . . . Have you been drinking?'

'A gin and tonic. Well, two. But I made them last half an hour.'

'Sorry, David.'

'Would you like a drink?'

'Yes please . . . Do you have Cinzano and lemonade?'

Campbell nodded and they went into the kitchen. Jean looked at their lunch. 'Gosh. That's nice, Dr Campbell. And I love strawberries.'

Campbell opened the bottle of Cinzano. 'What's the dose of this stuff?'

'For me, mainly lemonade . . . Did you get it specially?'

7

'Sort of. Saw you drinking it last night.'

'Thank you, David. And all this ... People who invite themselves to lunch at short notice just expect ...'

'What?'

'Straight to bed and a cup of coffee afterwards. If they're good.'

Campbell was taken aback. Lemonade spilled. 'Sorry, David. That sounds awful, but ... Mmm.' She kissed him then went across to the paper towel dispenser by the window. Campbell watched her hands as she mopped lemonade from the laminate worktop. She was wearing her wedding ring but not her engagement ring.

'I was going to give you until the afternoon to phone me ...' Jean was looking round for somewhere to put the soggy paper towels.

Campbell took them and stuffed them into an overfull fliptop bin. 'I was going to ring you as soon as I finished my clinic. It went on a bit ...' That sounded a lot less keen than he felt.

'I kept hanging round the Endocrinology Outpatients phone so the secretary wouldn't get there first and put you off.' Jean looked serious again. 'Then I thought I'd phone you so that if you'd changed your mind I would at least know. But early enough so we could have lunch today if you hadn't.'

'Thanks. And cheers.'

'Cheers, David. And I like Muscadet too.'

'So you'll have some lunch?'

Jean looked up at Campbell over her glass and smiled. There was a longish pause and she said, 'I like your flat.'

'It's all right. Bones found it. The girl who owns it's in Australia for two years ... I think she and Bones used to have something going.'

'So there's just the two of you?'

'Yes. Bones and me.'

'Is he around much?'

'Not really. And it's handy for the Institute.'

'Marchmont is, isn't it,' said Jean. Campbell wondered if he was being gently mocked. 'How many rooms have you got?'

'Two bedrooms. And a sitting room at the front. And this ...'

The kitchen was sunny and bright and, as Bones hadn't been back since the cleaning lady's day, quite tidy. It suddenly occurred to Campbell that Jean had been standing since she had arrived. He was still unsure about whether she wanted to eat anything, and even more unsure about how to proceed if she did not. She was looking round. 'Probably the same.'

'What?'

'Your flat. As ours. But the other way round.'

In circumstances of terrifying chastity, Campbell had visited Jean's flat about a year before. 'Yes. Probably.'

'But we don't have a big cupboard there.'

'It's quite useful.'

Jean took another sip of her drink. 'We're acting as if we've never met before and I've come to see if I want to buy your flat.' Campbell laughed but Jean did not. In a quieter voice she said, 'Are we making a mistake?'

'No.'

Jean put down her drink, took Campbell's hand and said, 'Come on then.'

They undressed without ceremony. Jean was naked first. She got into bed and lay on her back with the downie up to her chin. Campbell tossed his socks at the laundry basket and joined her. She was looking up at the ceiling and smiled as he wriggled in close to her. 'It's all exactly the same, but the other way round.'

After the party the previous evening Jean and Campbell had spent an agreeable hour together in her car. Despite repeated invitations she had not come up to his flat. Now she had, and they were in bed together, but they could not be said to have taken up where they had left off. Campbell lay wondering if a third gin and tonic might be the answer. Jean lay within his arms, working on him with the brisk and cheerful determination of someone preparing to inflict a minor but unpleasant procedure on a reluctant patient. Compliance remained poor.

'Don't worry about contraception,' she said suddenly. 'I've taken care of all that. In fact that's why I was late. I had to go home and get my diaphragm and I couldn't find it because we've been trying to have a baby for months. Then I found we'd run out of what my husband calls my homicidal cream so I had to rush out to a chemist's to get some, and then I tried to phone you to say I was coming but I'd be late but your phone kept being engaged so I thought you'd changed your mind.'

Campbell shook his head. Jean's hands, still much colder than they had been the previous evening, continued to work on him. The bedside clock flicked digitally on in red towards two o'clock, the time Campbell had arranged with Bertram for a final rehearsal of his presentation to Rosamund's research meeting at three.

The atmosphere of the previous evening remained elusive. At fourteen minutes past two Jean said, 'How about some lunch?' It

9

seemed a good idea. They got up and went naked back to the kitchen and stood looking at the lunch Campbell had prepared, and at each other. Jean went across to the window and then retreated rapidly. Fifty or sixty other Marchmont windows overlooked their sunlit domesticity.

'It's all right for men.' Jean picked up the pâté, the bottle of wine and the glasses. 'They're modest from the waist up. Let's have a picnic in bed.' Naked and from the back she was plumper than Campbell had imagined. He buttered some bread and followed her.

'Gosh, Dr Campbell . . . It must have been the pâté.' Jean opened her eyes and looked up at him. A few minutes after three o'clock a strange thing had happened. Just when Campbell should have begun his account of a year spent in the pursuit of greater understanding of the significance, if any, of faecal vitamins, more or less at the moment when Rosamund Fyvie would have introduced his presentation and taken out her pen and half a dozen of the little blank index cards she filled with minute and usually critical notes on all aspects of the working of her unit, a powerful inner calm had descended upon her junior research fellow.

Less than half a mile from the hospital, in a sunny Marchmont bedroom, Campbell had realised that his absence was a declaration by default, an informal but irrevocable termination of a futile research commitment. That was not something he could explain immediately to Jean, who would have been horrified at his irresponsibility, but its effect on him could scarcely have been more obvious. Calm, liberated and also by now a little drunk, he had suddenly regained his composure and his competence, and Jean had made the most of it.

Twenty minutes later, just about when Campbell should have been drawing his remarks to a close and admitting that his method was obsolete, his motivation minimal and the whole project a waste of time ('Difficulties remain, but the basic questions are challenging ones and further work is required when the necessary methodological refinements have been achieved . . .') Jean lay under him, flushed patchy pink to the waist and still breathing heavily, her hair damp with sweat and bedraggled by their exertions, her legs still crossed firmly over the small of his back. 'Coarse Ardennes,' he announced. 'From Marks and Spencers.'

'Mm.' Jean closed her eyes. 'And I think there's still quite a lot left.'

10

They got up and dressed at half past four, and walked together across the park to the Institute, not holding hands, not even touching, because there was a kind of pedestrian rush hour beginning which might include many people known to either or both of them. Campbell's elbows were sore, his thighs felt the way they had been after his first day's skiing and a pleasantly aching glow radiated out from his groin to his scalp and the tips of his toes. Bright-eyed and strangely garrulous, Jean walked beside him and told him things about herself that he was a little surprised to hear: her first affair, as a sternly practical schoolgirl; how she had not slept with her husband until just before they had married; then, in the context of an amused consideration of the small problem of the early afternoon, of how she had once, in the course of a relationship that had not come to much, spent a night of vain effort in a motel with walls so thin that her predicament was not only overheard by the occupants of the rooms on either side but was audibly discussed by them as well.

As they approached the Institute a man from the surgical side of the hospital who sometimes attended Rosamund's research seminars passed on his way home. A wave of residual guilt nudged Campbell, but only a little. Jean was walking so close that he could smell sex again, and even momentarily considered suggesting they go back to Marchmont, but a more serious commitment, and a feeling that Jean might start to sound a little more married if he suggested it, kept him walking in step with her towards the hospital.

Their first moment of awkwardness since just after three o'clock occurred when they reached the side entrance to the hospital. Campbell realised that he did not know why Jean, who lived only a few hundred yards from him on the other side of the park, was going back to the Institute so late on an afternoon when she had no clinical duties. His stint in the Intensive Care Unit started at five, and walking across together had been fun, but a touching farewell at the gate, from which large numbers of hospital folk were now emerging, would probably be a bad idea, especially as they had yet to discuss the delicate matter of where and how soon they might decently go to bed together again.

'I'm going back to Endocrinology Outpatients,' said Jean, answering his unspoken question. 'To get some books. I'm supposed to have spent the afternoon there swotting for membership.'

Campbell, who didn't want to be separated from her and still

11

wasn't sure how their affair was to continue, said, 'I'll walk down there with you.'

'No you won't,' said Jean. 'I'm going to escort you all the way to Intensive Care to make sure you don't get waylaid by some staff nurse with big eyes.'

Campbell laughed and they went through the stone arch leading from the park to the hospital grounds. They reached the main medical corridor and the door of the Intensive Care Unit still together, a future rendezvous still undiscussed. The corridor was an even sillier place to say goodbye than the gate from the park. A fat girl Campbell had once slept with out of lust and pity when he was drunk passed them, smiling at Campbell and looking pointedly at Jean.

'Who's that?'

'I think she works in clinical chemistry . . . Look, why don't you just come in for a couple of minutes? There's usually nobody about.'

The doctor on duty overnight for the Intensive Care Unit slept in a makeshift bedroom that functioned by day as an office. Someone had already effected the necessary transformation by opening out a narrow folding bed which now occupied almost half the available floor space. Jean sat down on it, wincing a little as she did so.

'Are you all right?'

'Just a bit . . . tender. Sitting down.'

'It's not a very comfortable bed.'

Jean bounced experimentally on it, once only and wincing again, and they both laughed out loud.

A year before, a few weeks after they had first met while working together on Creech's unit, Campbell had been on duty for the ICU and Jean, on duty for the ward and living in the residency, had come down to visit him late at night. Because of a misunderstanding involving several cans of beer and an ICU staff nurse, Campbell had been unable to entertain her, and had regretted it ever since. From the way she had behaved in his flat, and from her laughter now, it seemed that perhaps Jean had too.

'Not a very comfortable bed at all,' she said.

'Not in the least.'

'So it's just as well we didn't.'

'Quite.'

Jean reached up for his hands. 'Yours is much nicer.' She stood up, kissed him and said, 'I'll phone you tonight. Goodbye, David.'

'Goodbye.'

She kissed him again at the door, and went off down the corridor.

Rather than be seen standing drooling inanely, Campbell went back into the little bedroom. The smell of sex, and of Jean's perfume, still hung over the bed.

'Married?'

'No. Divorced, you could call it.'

'And you normally keep quite well?'

'Aye. Great. Usually.'

'And when did the pain start?'

'This afternoon. About half past four.'

'And what were you doing when the pain came on?'

There was no reply. Campbell leaned forward. The man had closed his eyes. There was a new rim of sweat on his upper lip. 'Are you all right?'

'Oh . . . Yes. Well . . . The pain's still there.'

Campbell glanced at the ECG monitor above the man's head. The tracing was no worse than before: a fair-sized anterior coronary thrombosis with no disorder of rhythm so far. The man looked worried, so Campbell checked his pulse, more in order to touch him than to add to the clinical facts, and said, 'The injection should work soon.'

'I hope so.'

'So what were you doing when the pain came on?'

The man hesitated. 'Does it matter?'

'Not a lot,' said Campbell. 'Did you notice anything else apart from the pain?'

'What sort of thing?'

'Sweating? Sickness? Difficulty breathing?'

'Oh. Yes.'

'Which?'

'Mainly the difficult breathing.'

'Anything else?'

'Well, I'm sweating now.'

'But no sickness?'

'No.'

'And the pain? Anywhere apart from the chest? Down your arm?'

'A bit. On the left. And a funny thing . . . Up my neck. And even into my teeth. I remember thinking, this is a funny way to get the toothache.'

'What was?'

'What I was doing when the pain came on.'

13

Campbell laid down his pen in the rather obvious way that was said to encourage frank divulgence by shy or embarrassed patients, and waited.

'But I definitely didn't feel sick.' The man relaxed and smiled. 'That's better. Your jag's working now.'

'Doctor Campbell . . .' A nurse stood at the door of the cubicle. 'Dr Campbell, there's a doctor on the phone for you.'

Campbell excused himself. Perhaps the best thing the patient could do for the moment was soak up his morphine. The next batch of questions in the standard Intensive Care protocol for coronaries was sometimes a little dispiriting. A man of fifty with acute chest pain might find himself listing a gloomy succession of relatives all of whom had died, at a similar or lesser age, of what he himself had now. That could wait without detriment for the duration of a phone call.

The nurse nodded towards a phone at the far end of the desk. 'Hello . . . Dr Campbell.'

'What are you playing at, you daft bugger?'

'Hello?'

There was a short, relieved burst of laughter, recognisable as Bertram's.

'Hello? Ronnie?'

'At least you've turned up for your ICU duty. Thought I was going to have to come in and do it, for the honour of the regiment. And it's the wife's yoga night too. Are you all right?'

'Fine, thanks.'

'So what happened?'

'Oh. Yes. That.'

'Yes, that. At half past two I thought, confident wee shit, can't be bothered running through it with old Ronnie, I hope all his slides come out upside down . . . But not turning up at three . . .'

'Yes, it was . . .'

'Rosamund drummed the fingers on the table and put on the small mouth. And the second speaker, the wee gas-liquid chromatography man with the terrible stutter, he hadn't turned up yet so we had five minutes of the fingers drumming and the small mouth . . . Seriously, son, you've dropped yourself in the faecal vitamins in a big way . . . Your testimonials are as good as in the mincer. Old Creech was nice about it, though. Said you were normally very reliable and you must have had a serious accident . . . Sounded as if he was going to do you a two-inch obituary for the *BMJ*.'

'That was nice of him.'

'So .. ? If you were just scared you can tell your uncle Ronnie. I even tried ringing your flat but it was off the hook. Anyway, young Campbell . . . Name's mud, ten brown stars and no ice cream for a week. Serve you right. Interview?'

'What?'

'Were you interviewing for another job?'

'No.'

'I think that's what Rosamund thought. So quite soon you could be . . . But don't ask her for a reference. Anyway, you've got four weeks to redeem yourself, if you've got a good excuse for this afternoon, that is. She's put you at the top of the bill for the first research seminar after she comes back from fun in the sun at the Nineteenth International Congress. Was it just cold feet?'

'No . . .' Just in front of Campbell one of the screens in the bank of ECG monitors attached to patients in the various cubicles showed a new abnormality. The heart rate had slowed down to around forty and an automatic alarm, a low-pitched buzzing sound, had been triggered. Campbell looked around for the staff nurse who had summoned him to the phone. 'Sorry, Ronnie. Someone's just slowed up a bit. I'd better have a look . . .'

'Right. Glad you're OK. Hope you have a quiet night . . .'

'Thanks, Ronnie.'

'. . . so you have a chance to think up some really good excuse. Cheers.'

Campbell put the phone down and checked the number on the monitor showing the bradycardia then walked quickly to the cubicle indicated. A staff nurse was injecting something into an IV line in the patient's arm. Without looking up she said, 'Point six of a milligram of atropine.' Campbell hesitated. 'Just write it up in the Kardex, doctor, thanks. We'll do the rest.'

'No, doc. My father's fine. Great for his age, in fact . . .'

'Your mother?'

'Away. Cancer. Ten years ago . . . So my father's on his own now.'

'Brothers and sisters?'

'None. So I have to . . .'

'Any aunts or uncles or other relatives have heart trouble?'

'Not that I know of . . . But to tell you the truth I hardly ever see them. There's just me and the old man in Edinburgh, so I try to get up there most days . . .'

'Mr Allen, just to get back to something I was asking about earlier

15

. . . What were you doing when the pain came on?'

'That's what I was trying to tell you, doc. Like I said, I'm on my own now, and the old boy's getting a wee bit frail, so I try to get up there most days. You know. Just to see he's all right . . .'

'So you were helping your father when the pain came on?'

'Well, not exactly . . . No. To let you understand, doctor . . .'

The phrase was one that Campbell had come to dread. It was generally a prelude to some vast detour in the clinical history: a chunk of autobiography, family politics, confession or self-justification that might swamp the main thread of inquiry for anything up to ten minutes. On this occasion, however, there was plenty of time. Campbell was on call for the Intensive Care Unit until eight o'clock the next morning, and so far no new cases were expected. It didn't even look as if the staff nurses were going to let him do very much anyway. Once more he put down his pen.

Compared with how he had looked when first admitted to the ICU half an hour before, Mr Allen was now pink, warm and relaxed. Morphine had helped him. Perhaps rattling on a bit about whatever was on his mind would help him some more. He took a deep breath. 'Like I was saying, doc, I'm on my own now . . . Have been for some years, and my health's pretty good . . .' He hesitated. 'You know what I mean, doc . . . Apart from this, like. And with being a postman I get a lot of walking, and I've got a wee garden. And I try to get up to see the old man most days . . .'

'So you were saying.'

Mr Allen hesitated. 'Did I mention that he's got a home help? Anyway, he has. Nice woman . . . Maybe a couple of years younger than myself. And she's really good with him. I should have said he's not the easiest person in the world to get on with, but she's very good with him. And today being Wednesday . . . Did I say he doesn't get out much? Anyway, an old pal from his work comes with his car and takes him out on a Wednesday, so if the home help happens to be there when I go up we generally have a cup of tea.'

'I see.'

'She's on her own as well . . . Separated maybe . . . Some kind of trouble. Anyway, it was a nice day, and we were sitting in the old man's kitchen and having this cup of tea . . . And one thing led to another and you know yourself how it is, doc. I mean, you're a man of the world. And here's me been divorced for maybe five years and what you might call deprived for a lot longer than that, and . . . Don't get me wrong, doc. She's a respectable woman . . . But . . .'

'So when the pain came on you were . . .'

'Exactly, doc.'

'Well, it happens. Not uncommon, so far as I know . . . But once you get better there's no reason to believe that . . .'

'There I was, doing fine. Really surprising myself. Mind you, I suppose it's not the sort of thing you . . . forget how to do . . . And then this pain started. In my neck at first, then in my jaw and teeth, like I said, then really bad across my chest. And another thing I noticed . . . If I sort of slowed up it went away a bit. At first anyway. Then it got really bad and Morag — that's her name, the home help — said, "Are you all right, Trevor?" I thought I was away, doc, but you know how it is. So I said I had this bit of pain in my chest . . . She was very good. Apparently they have some kind of training in first aid and all that, so she helped me lie down and then phoned for an ambulance. They were pretty good too. I mean, I'd hardly got my breeks up when they came.' Mr Allen took another deep breath. 'I thought I better tell you, doc . . . Not so much for anything you can do about it now, more from what you might call the research angle. I mean, you knowing all that might be a help to other people.'

Honest confession, good for the soul, thought Campbell, picking up his pen again. There was a pause and then Mr Allen smiled. 'And another thing, doc. A funny thing. When the pain was really bad — I mean when I thought I was away, you know — I found myself thinking, oh well. You know, like better than cancer and that sort of thing. I really wouldn't have minded. Apart from for Morag, and what my dad would think.'

When Campbell went back to the doctor's room it smelled strongly of macaroni and cheese. While he had been questioning and examining Mr Allen someone had been in, pushed the typewriter on the desk to one side and deposited in its place a tray with his evening meal. There was soup and a main course, both covered by aluminium lids, a side plate with two little biscuits and a triangle of processed cheese, and a cup of tea. The crockery was the thick, pale blue kind the Institute reserved normally for the exclusive use of patients. Nothing was hot. The tea was tepid, the macaroni just warm enough to be edible and the soup, greenish and pasty, not to be considered. Campbell sat down on the swivel chair at the desk and started on the macaroni and cheese. He was interrupted after three forkfuls by a staff nurse calling on the intercom to say that one of the visitors wanted to see him.

The visitor was a plump little woman in a good but unseasonal tweed coat. She had just been to see Mr Allen. She explained that his only relative was his father, who was unable to get out much, and she, not a relative but, as she put it, a friend of the family, was visiting on his behalf. Campbell escorted her into the little room next to the unit set aside to spare distressed and perhaps freshly bereaved relatives the more gruesome spectacles of acute medical care.

They sat down and Campbell said a few of the general things that could be said in the first six hours about any coronary patient who was pink and breathing.

'That's lovely, doctor. His father'll be that pleased. What a shock he got . . . Mr Allen — young Mr Allen, I mean — is normally such a fit man . . . And he got no warning at all. Apparently.'

'I see.'

'So he'll be all right now?'

'He's comfortable just now, as I said, and his condition's quite stable. As good as we could hope for at this stage.'

False teeth gleamed again and the visitor tightened her headscarf to go. 'Such a vigorous man, as a rule.' She turned as they left the bad news room and waved in the general direction of Mr Allen's cubicle, then departed, leaving large whiffs of a perfume Campbell would not immediately have associated with home helps.

'Hello? David?'

'Oh. Hello.'

'How are you?'

'All right.'

'Is this a bad time to phone?'

'No, not at all. It's quiet. One chap came in early, just after you went away, and there's been nothing much since.'

'That's . . .' Jean's voice was lost in background noise. From the sound of things she was calling him from the middle of a busy pub, which would have been rather unexpected.

'Sorry. Can't hear you.'

'I said that's nice. Then I said are you in that silly bed? So I didn't want to shout.'

'Where are you?'

'Giacomo's. A posh Italian place on George Street.'

Campbell, who knew without being told that Giacomo's was a posh Italian place on George Street, wondered what Jean was doing there late on a Wednesday evening.

'It's my birthday.'

'Happy birthday, Jean.'

18

'It's been the best for ages, thanks. And now my husband's taken me out for a posh dinner.'

'That's nice.'

'He's a nice husband . . . David, we haven't . . . We . . . Gosh, I'm missing you. It's silly, but I really am. I wish I was with you.'

There was a pause, with pub noises. Campbell remembered how Jean felt like against him. 'Mm. That would be nice.'

'When do you finish in the morning?'

'At eight. And I usually go back to the flat . . . Perhaps . . .'

'Yes. Quarter past eight. Gosh, David . . .'

'You should have told me this afternoon it was your birthday.'

'A bit beside the point. It was super and marvellous and I wish I was with you now. Even in that silly bed. So . . . See you tomorrow.'

'See you tomorrow.' Campbell started to say 'Happy Birthday' again, but Jean had hung up.

At half past six Campbell was roused from a sensual and athletic reverie about Jean by the shrill of the intercom. An orange light flashed and it gave forth a crackling summons to cubicle four. He threw on a shirt, slacks, and a white coat and crossed the corridor. In cubicle four, Mr Allen lay flat on his back. His pillows had been removed, his bed pulled out to the middle of the floor and its headboard taken away. His pyjama jacket was wide open and a staff nurse knelt on the edge of the bed, bending over him and jerking up and down as she compressed his chest. Another staff nurse, leaning over him from the far end of the bed, blew rhythmically into a clear plastic airway inserted into his mouth.

The patient's face, or what could be seen of it, was bluish-white and lifeless. The tracing on the monitor screen above told Campbell nothing: its jagged, racing line was an artefact of external cardiac massage. The staff nurse kneeling on the bed saw him looking and said, 'Asystole'.

Campbell nodded and went round to the bedside locker and a metal tray, normally covered by a neat white shroud, that contained a laryngoscope, an endotrachael tube and a thing like a polythene concertina that let you breathe patients who couldn't breathe for themselves. He checked the light in the laryngoscope and made sure the red rubber endotracheal tube fitted the tube on the concertina, then knelt on the floor beside the staff nurse at the head of the bed.

She removed the temporary airway then arched Mr Allen's neck and opened his mouth, so that Campbell's laryngoscope went in quite easily. So far so good. Getting a proper look at the vocal cords, parting them and sliding a tube down the trachea was the interesting bit, and probably easier if you were more in the habit of doing it than Campbell was. He squatted down, craning uncomfortably along the instrument into the mouth and throat of a man who was probably dead already.

If you were lucky, the patient did not vomit. You fiddled around with light and tube until you saw your target, then took a shot at it before it moved. Peering into the pink, glistening recesses Campbell saw something that looked like the larnyx, and pushed. Probably a hole in one, he thought, inflating the little cuff which made an airtight seal around the tube. The nurse handed him the polythene bellows to connect up, and pulled out a stethoscope to listen for air entering the chest.

'How long?' Campbell asked no one in particular.

'Coming up for two minutes,' said the second staff nurse, who was smearing more electrode jelly on to her metal paddles.

'Hello, Campbell . . . Didn't know you were on here tonight.'

'Oh, hello.'

The duty anaesthetist, a man from Campbell's year with whom he occasionally played tennis, had arrived quietly and was taking stock. 'How's it going?'

'Just going to shock him again.'

'Go right ahead.'

The staff nurse sniffed, applied her paddles and pressed the button. Mr Allen convulsed briefly, arching back and flopping down again perhaps an inch nearer the head of the bed. Wilson, the duty anaesthetist, watched thoughtfully then glanced at the monitor screen and shook his head. 'I suppose we could try some calcium,' he said without enthusiasm. 'What's that you've got up there?'

'Bicarb,' said the nurse doing external cardiac massage.

'What's the story anyway?'

'Previously fit postman,' said Campbell.

'Anterior transmural,' said the nurse on the bed. 'Sudden onset VF at six eighteen. Asystole after defibrillation . . . And we were a bit slow getting a tube into him.'

'Eyes?' Wilson was drawing up calcium solution from a vial.

Campbell looked at Mr Allen's pupils: huge, dark and unresponsive to direct light. 'They're up. Fixed, really.'

'This is a bit of a formality,' said Wilson. 'Excuse me.' The nurse pumping the patient's chest made way and he slid a four-inch needle between the fourth and fifth ribs on the left, pushed in the contents of his syringe and stood back to observe the effect on the monitored ECG trace. It remained flat. 'See what I mean?' He withdrew his syringe and tossed it expertly into the appropriate container on the floor. 'When they're like that you can't do a thing for them.'

The nurse who had been kneeling on the bed shook her skirt and apron back into place, mopped some stray hair from her face and smiled at the anaesthetist. Her colleague began disconnecting the various leads that had linked the patient to the machinery. Campbell looked round for an ophthalmoscope to confirm death formally by examining the blood vessels of the retina, wondering as he did so who was going to break the news to the dead man's father and the woman in the tweed coat, presumably the home help, who had visited him the previous evening.

No one asked Campbell to be the bearer of bad news. Later, as he left the unit, he asked the nurse in charge how these things were managed in the ICU. 'Simple,' she said. 'If they've got a phone you tell them the patient's got a lot worse and could they come in as quickly as possible . . . Then when they get here you say you're sorry, he's just away.'

'And if they don't have a phone?'

'The police. They're very good with tragic messages.'

At three minutes to eight the daytime ICU doctor appeared and at two minutes to eight, after the quickest handover he could remember, Campbell left the unit. When his time on duty offically expired he was clambering through a gap in the Institute's railings and heading out across the park towards Marchmont and Jean.

After the confines of the little office-bedroom and the windowless gloom of Intensive Care, morning in the park was clear and bright. A few early pedestrian commuters passed on their way into town and a middle-aged lady shrilled complicated threats at a terrier making advances to a thoroughly willing boxer bitch. Campbell walked briskly, confident that he was in good time for his appointment with Jean but hoping to fit in a quick shower before it too.

Though Campbell and Jean had known each other for more than a year and he had lusted after her more or less consistently throughout, recent developments had quite astonished him. They had met when she had joined Creech's unit as a house officer under his immediate supervision. Vaguely Christian and at first sight very married, she had spent hours in easy-going conversation with him

21

over coffee and lunch. Sometimes it had seemed to Campbell that some progression was inevitable, and only a matter of time; somehow it had never happened, and after the ICU incident Jean behaved as though it had never been even the faintest of possibilities, though they continued to spend as much time together having much the same sort of conversations.

After six months she had left for her present post in Endocrinology Outpatients, still at the Institute but far removed from Creech's unit. Campbell had seen her sometimes, in the hospital or simply around Marchmont, and they had exchanged civilities. He thought about her quite a lot, and would have liked to have seen more of her, but that would not have been possible without the crossing of that invisible line dividing chance from planned encounters.

So it would have remained, had not a chance meeting with Jean been followed shortly afterwards by a telephone call from the Institute's assistant chaplain, who had asked if Campbell could think of a female junior hospital doctor to help with a little project for which he had already recruited Campbell himself. That had been two weeks previously. Two nights previously, after a party at the assistant chaplain's, they had spent a hot and humid hour together in her car, disposing of a large proportion of the remaining barriers, and the following afternoon a few ounces of Marks and Spencers coarse Ardennes pâté had finished the job, to their mutual and hitherto continuing delight.

Campbell had his shower and decided there was no point in getting dressed again afterwards. Jean arrived at eight fifteen precisely. At quarter to nine they ate the rolls she had brought, and at nine they got up and went to work. Campbell was uncertain how she would feel about walking across the park together.

'Lots of people who aren't having affairs walk to work together,' said Jean. 'So it's all right. But we won't hold hands.'

'Fine by me.'

'We both work at the Institute and we used to work together. All very respectable. I'll just have to try not to look slept in and besotted.'

Campbell lived in a top flat in a crumbling Victorian tenement, and among his neighbours was a near contemporary in medicine. Getting downstairs and out on to the street was, he realised, the only potentially difficult bit. After that their being together could, as Jean had pointed out, have a number of respectable explanations. When they had walked a few yards down the street he must have looked obviously relieved, because Jean laughed. Campbell held her hand momentarily, and laughed too.

'And you don't have to worry about running into my husband and me having to introduce you.'

'Good.'

'He's on a train to Birmingham, perfectly happy and probably having a proper British Rail breakfast . . . I took him down to Waverley, then I thought I was going to be late for us so I drove like a maniac and turned right in front of a bus at some lights.' Jean smiled and laughed. 'The way he sometimes does. He was quite surprised. And then I ended up being so early for us I had time to go for rolls as well.'

'Thanks, Jean.' Campbell tried a rough calculation about return journeys to Birmingham, and wondered about seeing Jean again later that day.

'He's going to Cardiff. There's a friend of his in physiology there who's got a technique that might come in handy for his frogs.'

One of the few things that Campbell knew about Jean's husband, other than the fact that he was called Jim, was that he was doing a PhD in seasonal behaviour in amphibians: not something that Campbell had ever thought of as useful or significant. Cardiff, however, sounded even more like an overnight absence than Birmingham.

'Then they're going climbing for the weekend and he's coming back on Tuesday.'

Rather than throwing his briefcase in the air, hugging Jean and issuing an immediate invitation to her to come to his flat for the weekend, Campbell walked a little closer to her. They stopped at a kerb as a bus and a few straggling cars from the end of the rush hour roared past. Jean looked up at him, 'Gosh,' said Campbell. 'You should have told me . . .'

'I didn't know if you . . . I thought you might not want to see me again.'

'What?'

'You know . . . I thought you might just have wanted to screw me once or twice to show you could . . . And then . . .'

'No.' Campbell put his arm round her shoulders and drew her close. Her head leaned against his chin. A police car driven by a senior and immensely stern-looking policewoman swished past within three or four feet of them.

'So come round this evening,' said Jean into his tie. 'I'll cook for us.'

23

'Bad night in ICU, young Campbell?'

'Not particularly, thanks.'

'You look worn out. How was it?'

'Four patients, mainly OK, to start with. Then an admission who seemed fine but arrested this morning. Big anterior, went into VF and died.'

'All part of life's rich tapestry, I suppose ... I think I'm getting too old for ICU. Don't sleep as well as I used to in that ghastly room. I haven't told wee Norrie I might just suddenly take myself off his rota, but I'm going to.'

'Really.'

'Yes. The first time I clerk in somebody with a coronary who's younger than me, that's it. Off. Make way for you younger chaps who need the experience.'

'Thanks.'

Campbell and Bertram were in the sister's room of Creech's downstairs ward, having an early coffee. 'Thought I'd made it the last time I was on down there,' said Bertram through the crumbs of his ginger snap. 'Chap of twenty eight. Horrible collection of dead uncles and all that, but it turned out he'd just got pericarditis. Nice history. He'd fallen out of his wee sailing boat at Cramond the week before. Must have got the virus in a mouthful of Edinburgh sewage. So I'm on again a week on Tuesday.'

There was a long silence then Bertram said, 'You don't have to tell me what happened yesterday afternoon, son, but you'll really have to watch it when Rosamund gets back. Said something about you obviously having got the day of the meeting wrong, but she was bloody angry. Went off muttering something about redeeming yourself if you can to get some biopsy correlation even at this late stage.'

'I know.'

'Done many?'

'Biopsies?'

'Yes.'

'A few.'

'Fraser'll give you a hand.'

'Great.'

'In fact he was looking for you earlier. About quarter past nine. Seems he had one of the patients for his study all trussed up and ready for you.'

That morning Campbell had found on his desk, on top of the layer of unopened *BMJs*, a manilla envelope containing a detailed memo from Dr Rosamund Fyvie and a clutch of photocopies of learned articles to which it referred. The memo made depressing reading, which was why Campbell had gone early for coffee. His supervisor had dismissed the sporadic efforts of the first twelve months of his study in a few paragraphs, particularly deploring his failure to persist with attempts to obtain fresh samples of gut mucosa from the Institute's various operating theatres.

Those early weeks, when Campbell had spent hours waiting about in what Hadden had called the kebab squad, hanging around ghoulishly for operations that rarely delivered the goods, were not to be repeated. Instead, Campbell was to take biopsies of his own from patients undergoing investigations for another study, carried out mainly by Fraser Ratho, whose co-operation Rosamund had already enlisted, and who was so enthusiastic about helping that Campbell had already missed his first specimen.

'Cheer up, young Campbell,' said Bertram. 'There'll be dozens more soon. Fraser's just had a bollocking quite like yours. Finger out for the next four weeks or nice Dr Fyvie will be very, very cross. So he's scared shitless. You know the routine. "Job in Wigan you probably ought to apply for . . ." And "Have you thought of geriatrics, Dr Ratho . . ? Lots of openings there." So you'll soon have plenty of biopsies to correlate with anything she tells you they're supposed to correlate with, and be home and dry. Might even be an MD in it . . .'

Campbell finished his coffee, in order to be out of sister's room by the time Fraser Ratho came for his.

'Another thing, young Campbell . . . The assistant chaplain was in earlier, looking for you. Said it wasn't urgent but could you get in touch with him today.' Campbell nodded. Bertram sat back. 'You want to watch it, you know. Unexplained afternoons off and visitations from the clergy. People will be starting to talk about you. More coffee?'

'No thanks.'

'Go on. You look as if you need it.'

'No thanks, Ronnie.' Campbell got up to go.

'And this afternoon?'

'What?'

'What are we supposed to say if anyone's looking for you this afternoon? Choir practice followed by the young people's prayer circle and licking envelopes for Christian Aid . . .?'

'Yes,' said Campbell. 'That sort of thing, more or less.'

'Cheers, son.'

'Cheers.'

Campbell went back to his desk in the research fellows' room and re-read the memo from Rosamund, glanced through her latest batch of reprints on faecal vitamins and put them to one side with a firm resolve to read them after lunch. One, from the Tallahassee group, ran to seven or eight pages and had been heavily underlined and asterisked. Campbell checked back to the memo to confirm that the study it reported was the one that Rosamund had proposed he should replicate, and put it on top of the heap. It was still only twenty past ten.

'Hello? Andrew Gordon speaking.' The assistant chaplain had answered his bleep with commendable speed.

'David Campbell. I believe you were trying to get in touch with me earlier.'

'Yes, David. Thanks for ringing back. I don't know if you've been in touch with Jean Moray recently . . .' There was a longish pause, and the assistant chaplain continued. 'Anyway, she may have mentioned something about interviews.'

'Yes. She did say . . .'

'Well, it's all a bit more definite than it was, so the feeling is that we should get on with things. Dickie Dunn's away, and he's away for another three weeks so we probably shouldn't hang about till he gets back . . . The advert for the main job was in the *Times Higher Ed. Supp.* two weeks ago and Prof Hamilton says we should just go ahead.'

'Prof Hamilton?'

'The other grant-holder. Professor of Practical Ethics . . . No reason you should have heard of him but a perfectly decent old stick. He's got a couple of people in mind for the interview board, so they could do you, me and Jean and the person from nursing some day next week.'

'Sounds fine.'

'You're still quite keen?'

'Yes. Yes indeed.'

'Good . . . Probably Wednesday, just after lunch, so as to cause minimum disturbance for all our busy doctors. To be confirmed Monday, if that's OK.'

'Sounds fine.'

'Oh . . . And if you could perhaps get in touch with Jean . . . I don't want to put you to any trouble but I've had no luck yet with her extension, and I'm down at Calvin College for the rest of the day. Interviews probably next Wednesday, early afternoon.'

26

'I'll pass that on.'

'Thanks, David. Even if you just leave a note on her desk . . .'

'No problem . . . Oh. Andrew . . .'

'What?'

'Where?'

'Heavens, yes. Yes. Well, why not in the Institute? Save time for most people. I'll try and book the boardroom.'

'Fine.'

'Thanks, David.'

After lunch Campbell took a leisurely stroll in the sun, getting as far as George Street and visiting several bookshops in what turned out to be a search for some kind of belated birthday present for Jean. The problem was solved when, prompted by a recollection of a strange enthusiasm of hers from one of their long chaste conversations over coffee last summer, he found a recent biography of Edith Piaf, a hardback with her lyrics, and translations of them, and grainy black and white pictures of Paris in the twenties and thirties. Rather than write something in it that might provoke awkward questions later, he found a silly birthday card, and then spent quite a lot of the afternoon thinking both about what he might write in it and about Jean generally.

Campbell shared the research fellows' room with five others, all of them junior members of the clinical and research team headed by Henry Creech and Rosamund Fyvie. Of the six desks, all garnished with the journals, reprints, computer printouts and rough drafts that denoted higher learning in medical circles, Campbell's was perhaps the least impressive. He was, after all, the most junior of the occupants, and might also, if things turned out as he intended, be the first to leave.

When he had first taken up his research appointment, he had found the state of the other desks somewhat daunting. Only after several weeks had he realised that the occupant of the most impressive desk of all, in the corner with the best view out of the window and laden even in its barest areas several inches deep in assorted papers, was simply never around. Bill Dempster, whose desk ran a close second, was almost as elusive and only the tidy girl by the door seemed to use the room more than Campbell did himself.

That afternoon he was alone. Thoughts of Jean, the birthday card and the Tallahassee paper filled the time comfortably as the patch of sunlight swung across floor and desks towards three o'clock and tea. In sister's room in the upstairs ward Creech was in expansive form and Campbell lingered to the end of his account of the Japanese surrender in Singapore. ('Of course there was a lot of interest in which way *their* guns were pointing, but to tell you the truth I didn't actually see any of them . . .')

By four fifteen Campbell had concluded that the Tallahassee group, twelve of whom were named as authors of the paper, probably deployed three times that number of laboratory staff, together with equipment ('partially funded from US Federal Grant KX-405604-589') on a Manhattan Project scale. More than ever he felt like leaving them to it, their methods unemulated, their views unchallenged.

He was preparing to go when the houseman from the female ward came in. He looked round then asked Campbell, 'Is Bill away?'

'Sorry. Haven't seen him all day.'

'Dilys?'

'I think she's taken a few days off.'

'Well . . . It's about one of Rosamund's patients . . . So can I just ask you?'

'Fine.' Campbell, officially cutting back on his clinical work to concentrate on research, still kept in touch with Dr Fyvie's in-patients, standing in for Bill's various absences and often acting as second on call overnight.

'Mrs Grozninsky.'

'Yes . . .'

'In the ward. Gastric carcinoma.'

'I know. And we're making her comfortable.'

'We were.'

'Were?' Mrs Grozninsky was a woman in her sixties, a widow from an Edinburgh slum, Polish only in that she still used her late husband's name. A few months before, Campbell had seen her as an outpatient and organised the investigations that had determined the cause of her weight loss. After her barium meal she had gone to surgery, but simply been opened and closed again, her stomach cancer beyond hope of cure.

'Her son wants to see somebody in charge,' said the houseman. 'And nobody else is about.'

Campbell put on his white coat again and followed him upstairs to the female ward. 'Didn't know she had a son. Came up to outpatients with her daughter, I think. Didn't mention anyone else.'

'Well, he's here, and he's not very pleased.'

At outpatients, when the result of the barium meal had been

explained to her, the daughter had cried and then said that her mother had known she was dying because she had had hiccoughs lasting more than three days. 'Some daft thing my dad must have told her. He was Polish and kind of superstitious.' Campbell had wondered about that and later mentioned it to Bertram, who assured him that all Poles thought that, and it was sometimes a cheap way of diagnosing cancer spreading to involve the diaphragm.

Since then, Mrs G, as the nurses called her, had lost more weight and become progressively weaker, and now — another and perhaps even more reliable sign of the approach of death — occupied the first bed on the left as you went into the ward.

Her son was a squat man in his middle thirties, deeply tanned and wearing a crumpled powder-blue suit, a silk shirt and a tie that reminded Campbell of an amateur production he had once seen of *Guys and Dolls*. He was seated at his mother's bedside, facing not her but the entrance of the ward. He got up as Campbell and the houseman approached, and extended a hand to Campbell.

'Chief of the service, huh?'

'I'm sorry . . .?'

'You the guy in charge, huh? Of this lady's case.'

The man's accent, strange in his opening phrase but in general transatlantic, became odder the more he said. His manner too was changing, and Campbell had the impression it would become more suspicious if not frankly hostile when his own status in relation to the patient was disclosed. 'I'm sorry, Mr Grozninsky . . .'

'Groves . . . Buddy Groves. Of Galveston, Texas, U S of A.'

'Oh. I thought you were . . .'

'Mrs Grozninsky is my mother. But my name . . .' He smiled, as though by way of explanation, '. . . is Groves. Dr . . .?'

'Campbell.'

'Dr Campbell, I took the plane just as soon as my li'l sister told me mom was, uh, in a terminal condition. With her tumour. I couldnae have come quicker.'

'I see.' At least the accent problem was solved. The man, originally half Polish and half Scottish, was now doing his best to be one hundred per cent American.

'And you're in charge of her case, Dr Campbell, huh?'

'The consultant's actually Dr Fyvie . . .'

'You gonna contact him? I just came near four thousand miles to see my mom. And I ain't too happy.'

'Is there something I could help with?' said Campbell, only too

29

aware that Rosamund Fyvie was now well on her way to Hawaii.

'Look.' Mr Groves nodded towards his mother. 'You call that terminal care, huh? In a public ward, see? An' no lines, no monitor, no nothin'.'

'So far as we know she's very comfortable now . . .' Campbell moved towards the patient but Mr Groves blocked his path. 'An' this Fyvie guy, is he a regular oncologist? Look, Dr Campbell, why don't you just cut the crap and call him the noo, eh?'

'It's not as easy as that. Dr Fyvie is . . .'

'Don' get me wrong, doc. I know this stuff from Charlea's mom, that's the mither in law, dyin' from her tumour in the Oncology Centre, Galveston. My wee sister tried to tell me it's all OK here, but I say it's socialised medicine, you gotta watch them. So I come. Hell, I come clean with you, doc. I gotta know all this stuff. I mean, I'm captain of the rescue squad, you know?'

That did not mean much to Campbell, and perhaps he should have let the man go on talking. Instead he tried to soothe him. 'I've actually talked to your sister several times, Mr Groves . . .'

'Now you talk to Buddy. Straight. Is she gonna make it, doc? An' how much chemo's she gettin'?'

'You mean chemotherapy?'

Mr Groves laughed. 'At least you heard of it, Dr Campbell.'

'Unfortunately, by the time the diagnosis was made, there was spread . . .'

'So? You missed the diagnosis, huh? You don't have to say any more, doc, if you don't want to . . . Maria!'

The man was looking over Campbell's shoulder towards the door. He stopped talking and hurried past to embrace a small, worn-looking woman Campbell recognised as Mr Grozninski's daughter.

'Maria, hen . . .' He hugged her and slapped her shoulders. 'You're lookin' great.'

'Woyzek, you came to see us . . . Mama, look who's here . . . Mama.'

They turned together to Mrs Grozninski, who was lying back, paler than she had been, with her mouth open and her eyes half closed. Campbell stepped quickly past them to draw the curtain round her bedspace. 'I'm sorry, Mr Groves . . .'

The daughter shrieked and fell forward to clutch the shrivelled figure on the bed. Mr Groves shouted, 'Momma!', then he too huddled over, grasping the head as though to kiss his dead or dying mother. To Campbell's horror he did not, but tore the false teeth from her mouth, clamped his face to hers and delivered a mighty

30

blast of mouth to mouth resuscitation. His sister clutched frantically at his jacket but was ignored. With the heel of his right hand he pummelled the chest with short, powerful strokes. There was a horrible crunch as several ribs gave way.

'Woyzeck! Woyzeck! Dinnae!'

'Mr Groves . . .'

A staff nurse appeared, summoned by the disturbance at a bed where all had been peace moments before. She comforted the daughter, and completely ignored Mr Groves. It seemed a good idea. Gradually his resuscitation efforts waned. He stood up, looked around at the houseman, his sister, Campbell and the staff nurse, then wiped a streak of vomit from his face and wept.

It was some time before order was restored. While the houseman certified the death of Mrs Grozninski, Campbell and the staff nurse took the son and daughter away from her bedside and into another of the little rooms set aside in the Institute for the tidy management of distressed relatives. Some tea appeared and the staff nurse went away, leaving Campbell mainly to listen as the daughter explained how her mother had wanted to die 'to be with my father' and the son, his transatlantic accent now quite threadbare with emotion, related how he couldnae have got there ony quicker.

On his way across to Jean's flat with the Piaf book, the birthday card, a bunch of freesias and a bottle of the Muscadet she said she liked, Campbell wondered if he was overdoing it, and decided that if he was it didn't matter. He had cared a lot about her for a long time, and had until very recently never been in a position to do anything more for her than make the occasional cup of coffee. He rang her doorbell, still a little self-conscious.

He need not have worried, because Jean too had made visible efforts. She came to the front door in a dress he hadn't seen before, looking somehow more formal than he had expected, with her hair a little different and even some eye make-up. That and his armful of presents and the way she took them conjured up for Campbell images of a kind of evening — a bright little young-marrieds dinner party with proper conversation and the wedding-present china — very different from the one he had been anticipating.

It must have showed. Jean smiled then burst out laughing and then Campbell did too. He hugged her, squashing the freesias, and she said, 'Yes, I thought it would be nice to have the Bertrams round to meet you, and of course the Creeches. But you're the first to arrive, Dr Campbell, and thank you for the beautiful flowers . . .'

31

He followed her into the kitchen, still laughing.

'That's your G and T. It's ready because I knew you'd be on time.'

'Thanks . . . It's nice to see you.'

'Mm. Ages since this morning. I only had one patient all day and I sat not swotting for membership and daydreaming about you.'

'Same here.'

'Mine had thyroid acropachy and I was pleased as anything because I'd just read about it.'

It would have been against the spirit of the occasion to have said 'Mine died', and even more so to have gone into details. Campbell decided he would tell Jean about Mrs G later, when a suitable opportunity arose. 'That was clever.'

'Yes, it's nice to know about things.'

'Cheers.'

'Cheers.'

Campbell sat down on the window bench and watched Jean doing fussy things with a sauce. On his previous visit, sitting in the same place, he had watched her butter crumbly homemade gingerbread, and a large labrador had glowered at him for some minutes before ambling off to lie menacingly across the bedroom doorway. On this occasion it was not to be seen, and perhaps the fact that it had not barked either was of some significance.

'Your dog . . ? Sally?'

'Got herself pregnant, silly bitch. So she's gone to stay with Jim's parents. But she was really getting too big and bouncy for this place even before she got into trouble.'

'Oh.' Campbell took another mouthful of gin and tonic and realised that Jean made them for him exactly as he made them for himself. 'I was sort of expecting her.'

'I could have strangled her,' said Jean. 'The last time.'

'Really?'

'Yes really.'

'Gosh.'

'And you didn't even touch me.' Jean came over, still carrying her wooden spoon. 'You were awfully shy.'

'Sorry.'

'But you're not now.'

'I might be,' said Campbell, solemnly over his gin. Jean looked concerned. 'When the Creeches and the Bertrams arrive.'

She kissed his forehead. 'Just us. And I've wanted to cook for you for ages.'

Campbell watched as Jean rinsed her spoon and put it in the

dishwasher, poured herself a token dry sherry and unwrapped her book. She was surprised and pleased and said, 'Gosh, David, that was clever. I saw it somewhere, or reviewed or something and wanted it, but wouldn't have bought it in a million years, or until it was a paperback. Thank you very much.'

They ate avocado with shrimps, then trout with Jean's amazing sauce and rice and broccoli, then zabaglione, maintaining throughout a kind of affectionate formality, as though making up for the omission of such an occasion before they had gone to bed together, and between them — Campbell more, Jean less — drank a bottle of white wine rather better than the one he had brought.

The trout was puzzling. In his distant youth, Campbell had fished with minimal success for brown trout in rain-swollen upland streams. Not much got thrown back, and the taste of these little fish, fried only hours after being caught, had set standards that restaurant trout, the few times he had tried them, had failed to achieve. Jean's were proper trout, not fishy blotting paper, and he asked about them.

'They're from the deep freeze. Jim catches dozens of them.'

Campbell realised that he knew more about the delinquent dog than he did about his, so to speak, absent host. At least he had met Sally. The husband, conveniently provident, conveniently away, was an altogether more puzzling creature, not least in the way Jean talked about him and behaved in his absence.

They had coffee and began to tidy up, and decided to go back to Campbell's flat for the night. There was one slight problem about that, at first sensed rather than discussed. It seemed to Campbell that a telephone call might reasonably be expected from Cardiff. After all, that was what he, in similar circumstances, would have done as matter of routine husbandly concern. The problem remained undefined, but moves towards leaving for Campbell's flat were deferred, without discussion, by a distinct slowing of the process of tidying up.

Eventually Jean looked sharply at the phone and said, 'Come on, husband.' To Campbell's surprise it rang. There was a short, rather general conversation, neither cold nor particularly affectionate, then Jean put the phone down.

'Does that happen often?' Campbell asked.

'That? With the phone .. ? Oh, sometimes ... David, will you feel terribly moved-in on if I bring my toothbrush?'

'Please do.'

They walked through summery darkness rich with the malty,

33

Edinburgh smell of brewing that drifted up the hill from Fountainbridge. They held hands and looked up at the ceilings of Marchmont, an astonishing display of the vigour, inventiveness and occasional riotous bad taste influencing matters of decor in a first-mortgage area. Not quite hurrying, they reached Campbell's flat and went straight to his bedroom. 'I'm not sure if I approve of single men having double beds,' said Jean, 'but I'm glad you do.'

Next morning, as they walked across the park to work, Campbell remembered his telephone conversation with the assistant chaplain. 'He said the boardroom, probably, and some funny little committee would interview him, you, me and the person from nursing. All a bit of a charade, but Dickie seemed to think it would be a good idea.'

'That'll be nice. I'll get to see you during working hours.'

'Who's the person from nursing?'

'I don't think it's definite yet, but it's probably going to be Anna Affleck.'

'Who?'

'She's a sort of thinking nurse. I know her vaguely from school. Andrew says she's quite keen to be involved.'

'Is she horrible?'

'Just a bit . . . bossy, organising. You know. But Andrew says she's very keen.'

'And just one?'

'One what?'

'Nurse .'

'Well, there'll be more when he gets his committee going. Why? Do you have someone in mind, Dr Campbell, for when you get bored with me?'

Campbell was hurt, and turned towards Jean and saw she didn't mean it. 'No. Because I won't.' She reached across to him and touched his hand but did not hold it.

'I must say I'm awfully pleased with the support I've had from Dr Fyvie. Especially recently. Don't you find that, David? She just seems to sense when you need that little bit of extra encouragement, and there she is, telling you it's basically a tremendously important project and how easy it is to lose sight of that in the day to day . . . hassles, if you know what I mean.'

Campbell nodded, which was a mistake. Ratho put down his coffee cup and looked at him as though he were about to invite him to come to Jesus now. 'She's a wonderful supervisor and I've never been more aware of that than I have been over the last few weeks. I think it's because she's done so much research herself, so she's completely aware of what an essentially . . . lonely business it can sometimes be.'

That sounded a little suspicious. Rosamund Fyvie's reputation was that of one who had explored every frontier of scientific plagiarism. And having acquired someone else's ideas she did not even have the grace to do the necessary lab work herself; Bertram had quoted her as once saying that the most important research question of all was the question of who was going to do it for you.

'I know you've had one or two . . . little difficulties, David. We all do, and we're tremendously sympathetic, and that's why I'm so glad that my IBS study has so much to offer to your line of investigation. Even at this late stage.'

'Yes,' said Campbell. 'Rosamund left a note saying something about that. I really should have got in touch with you earlier.'

'I know how it is, David.'

When Campbell had gone for coffee, even earlier than on the previous day, Ratho had been lying in wait. Another suitable patient was threatened, and as Campbell had not yet found another job it looked very much as though he would be compelled to inflict an unnecessary and sometimes uncomfortable procedure upon an innocent citizen.

'What exactly's involved in the IBS study?'

'No need to be fierce about it, David. It's simply taking a gentle look at pressure and volumes in the large bowel for what is after all a very important condition. Dr Fyvie's quite keen to establish the method. I believe the pharmaceutical industry would have quite a lot to offer any group that could really evaluate a therapeutic response in IBS.'

'So what do you actually do?'

'As I said, David, pressures and volumes, with a bit of a look at anal function too. We're really getting quite consistent results now.'

'In volunteers?'

'Volunteers are always welcome. Quite important to document normality. But mainly it's patients. From the CDOP clinic.'

'How do you look at anal function?' Campbell asked partly because he was curious, having recently come across a little book about a Frenchman who could break wind to the tune of *The Flight of the Bumblebee*, and partly because Ratho was becoming visibly uncomfortable under interrogation, in a way that at least had the

35

merit of putting off for the moment specific arrangements about pulling little bits out of people's insides.

'We're using SNST, actually.'

'Oh.'

'I'm surprised you haven't heard of it,' said Ratho. 'Standard technique.'

'Really?'

'Sacral nerve stimulation test.'

'Oh . . . What do they stimulate?' Ratho turned pink. Having lost the last couple of points, Campbell felt he might be regaining the upper hand. 'It sounds quite interesting . . .'

Ratho took a last mouthful of coffee and put his cup down with a bang. 'If you took your work a little more seriously and got down to it and did some biopsies you might find out.' He stood up and turned to leave. 'I think you should know that Dr Fyvie asked me to make a special effort to bale you out, David. These were her exact words. But I'm beginning to think it might not be worth the trouble.'

Campbell finished his coffee, and had another one when Bertram and the downstairs houseman joined him, and then went back to the research fellows' room where, for the first time in his career, he perused the Situations Vacant pages of the *BMJ*.

'Hello? David? Andrew Gordon here. Sorry to bother you at home.'

'It's all right.'

'I wondered if perhaps we ought to get together . . . Before the weekend if possible. Lunch tomorrow?'

'Sounds fine.'

'I've tried to get in touch with Jean. Missed her at work and she seems to be out for the evening. Really, the three of us ought to get together, just to go over what we're trying to do, before the interviews. And we ought to come to some sort of decision about the nursing side of things. So lunch, at the club might be best. And I'll try and get hold of Jean tomorrow morning. One o'clock?'

'Fine, Andrew. See you then.'

Campbell put the phone down and went back to the kitchen, where Jean was on her second Cinzano and lemonade.

'I turned the butter down, David. It was beginning to smoke.'

'Thanks . . . Andrew wants us all to have lunch together tomorrow. He'll ring you at work about it in the morning.' Campbell returned to his mushrooms, perhaps looking thoughtful.

'It's all right.'

'What?'

'I'm not supposed to know till he phones me. I'll remember. I'm really getting quite good at all this. And at lunch I'll not kiss you or hold hands or anything. Or remind you to get some potatoes on the way home. Or straighten your tie, even if it needs it.'

'Fine.'

'I'll do my best. Gosh. I love you.'

Andrew Gordon, assistant chaplain to the Institute, had been vaguely known to Campbell in his time there as a clinical student. They had become better acquainted in the course of his year as a houseman. Andrew, younger and less forbiddingly religious than his full-time superior, had been suggested when the principal speaker lined up for a Residency mess dinner had withdrawn at the last minute. Campbell rang him and he had agreed immediately, and only a few hours later delivered a ceremonial ode on the fifty or so years' worth of Residency group photographs displayed around its lower floors.

Beginning in the manner of Betjeman ('Far away beyond the toilets, stretching to the brink of doom . . .'), and breaking into Tennysonian ('Half a year, half a year, half a year backwards . . .') for its centre section, it had ended with a slightly fleshly flourish in the manner of Burns. The piece was well received, and when Campbell congratulated him Andrew had said simply that it was fun to do something that was a bit more of a challenge than writing sermons.

They had remained in touch, occasionally lunching together. Andrew held a joint appointment, half time at the Institute and half time at Calvin College, preparing intended Church of Scotland ministers for the rigours of parish life ('A nice balance. Makes you dreadfully sceptical about both professions.'), and over the previous few months had been in the process of setting up what he called 'a loose sort of study to look at some interesting things'.

Andrew, tall, thin and less solemn than he looked, was sitting with Jean in the lounge of the club when Campbell arrived a few minutes after one o'clock, apologising for his lateness.

'It's all right. Busy doctors and all that . . . Jean and I had just been trying to sort out the nurse thing. Basically we have to have a nurse on the core group or they'll get paranoid, but nobody really springs to mind . . . The problem is that academic nurses aren't real nurses and real nurses can't think.'

'Why not one of each?' said Jean. 'If you're having two doctors.'

'They'd fight,' said Andrew.

'Really?'

'I think so. And the core group should really be as small as possible. That, and work well together.' As Andrew explained why, Campbell glanced at Jean, who was so convincingly distant that he wondered if something had gone wrong. She shot him a tiny smile and went straight back to her serious listening face. '. . . compatible with flexibility. Don't you think so, David?'

'Um. Yes.'

'So one nurse. Anna. And for the larger group, you really can't avoid Brenda.'

Campbell knew of no unavoidable nurses called Brenda, but it sounded as if he ought to soon, so he said 'Who?' and listened as carefully as Jean appeared to be doing.

'Brenda Boylan. Typical heavyweight academic nurse. Australian. Ex-nun, of course, and a militant feminist lesbian.' Campbell was taken aback. 'Communist too, I hear,' said Andrew. 'But in this job you're supposed to think the best of people.'

They went for a pre-lunch drink. Campbell and Andrew had sherry and Jean a tomato juice. They spent a few more minutes in the lounge, talking generally about the composition of the larger group, then went into the dining room. Campbell held the door open for Jean, who contrived to brush her hand against his as she passed.

Over lunch Andrew expanded on his ideas about the proposed group: 'Big enough so it's still workable even if half the busy doctors sometimes don't turn up, but not so big that everyone doesn't get to know everyone else. And sufficient in the way of divergence to have a genuine discussion, but enough in common so they at least understand each other. And it's got to be fun or people just won't come. So a dinner every meeting. And claret, I suppose. There are precedents. Our illustrious forebears more or less swam in it.'

Only towards the end of lunch did they discuss the interviews, and even then only because Jean raised the subject.

'Heavens, yes. Well, it's just that Dickie Dunn thinks you're as well to do it that way. Maintains the academic ideal of objectivity but all perfectly fixable, were his exact words. And unfortunately he's in Hong Kong. But some sort of little committee would go down well both with the sponsoring departments and with funding bodies, so Prof Hamilton's agreed to get something together for Wednesday.'

'Is there anything I should read up on?' Jean asked.

'Shouldn't think so. You're both in it simply as actual doctors, to help me with the more medical bits, and . . . be available. We'll probably call you research associates. Is that all right . . ? But you won't have to do any research.'

That seemed all right. They finished lunch and Andrew took his leave in bright sunshine on the steps of the club, to head north for his afternoon's duties at Calvin College. ('It's called a seminar on communicating with patients. I tell them not to shout at the old ladies.') Jean and Campbell, blamelessly together in broad daylight, walked back to the Institute, as colleagues might.

'It's funny,' said Jean. 'Just sitting near you, I can practically feel you inside me.'

'Good. I thought you'd forgotten all about me.'

'And it's still ages till bedtime.'

'Then we've got all weekend.'

Jean went quiet and in response Campbell started to worry about certain things: how, for instance, Jean was to maintain reasonable accessibility to telephone calls from Wales; what would happen if Bones returned to the flat unexpectedly; whether (since a whole weekend in a small Marchmont flat might in the event turn out to be a little limiting) they could take a chance on going out in daylight together perhaps once; and whether or not Jean was worrying about the same things.

'Andrew's nice,' she said eventually.

'Very relaxed about everything.'

'He is.'

'What did he say when he first talked to you about all this?'

'Oh, we just chatted for a while. About lots of things. I've known him for ages. He said you'd suggested me and when you did he realised he should have thought of me for himself.'

'Really?'

'Yes. I've known him for ages.'

'Didn't know that.'

'Yes. Since I was a wee girl. Well, since I was in youth fellowship. He was our assistant minister. So I thought it was all because of that. And then he said you'd probably be in it too. So then I thought, it would be nice to see him again. And then he said you'd suggested me, and I thought, gosh. Then when he said the big group would probably start with a residential weekend I thought we'd probably . . . really see each other properly then. And then the party. So thanks for suggesting me.'

'Don't mention it.'

Jean reached across and dug Campbell in the ribs. 'And in the car was awful. I've hardly ever necked in cars and I've never ever in my whole life been so worked up and not. And normally — I mean for married people — that just doesn't happen.'

'You should have come up. I kept asking you to.'

'I nearly did.'

'Why didn't you?'

'Because I might never have gone home. Home home, I mean.'

There was another silence. When they reached the Institute Jean said, 'Come down to Endocrinology Outpatients for a coffee. I've got all the stuff.'

Campbell hesitated, on grounds of discretion rather than pressing duty.

'Come on,' said Jean. 'You could be telling me what to read for membership. Or seeking a second opinion on a difficult endocrinological case. And I know what you usually do on Friday afternoons.'

Endocrinology Outpatients was empty and quiet. Jean's room, at the end of a short corridor floored with old-fashioned squeaky linoleum, looked out over an unused tennis court to the back of the maternity pavilion. As she stood waiting for the kettle to boil Campbell moved behind her and held her, then slid his hands under her waistband and downwards, stroking her and at the same time mouthing the back of her neck. 'Don't, David. I'll want you to screw me and I don't want to be screwed here.' She opened her legs a little, leaned back against him and said 'I've only got plastic milk from a packet. Would you rather have it black? Oh . . . That's nice. Someone might come in.'

'We'd hear them.'

'We might not.'

'We would,' said Campbell, 'unless they took their shoes off. Or walked on their hands.'

Jean giggled. 'Really quick then.'

They made love really quickly, standing up, with Jean lunging against Campbell for seconds only, and the kettle boiling just as they finished together. She pulled his hair and bit his neck, then sat unbelieving on her desk, her skirt still round her waist. Campbell made the coffee. Jean got up slowly and found a bunch of paper hankies to wipe up the little spermy puddle she had left. 'Gosh, Dr Campbell. You're bad for me. And my desk.'

Campbell handed her a coffee, which she declined with a gesture, instead reaching downwards. 'So I'm going to put my knickers on again right away, before you start getting ideas about me.'

With decency restored, having coffee together seemed so

resoundingly respectable that Campbell lingered in Jean's office for fully half an hour. They talked about the examination for the first part of the Membership of the Royal College of Physicians, a hurdle Campbell had passed and for which Jean was preparing. Campbell's approach, which had been to delay registering for the exam and hence paying the fee till the last possible moment, then spending the remaining four weeks doing little except reading textbooks and attempting old question papers, did not appeal to Jean, but their choice of books was remarkably similar.

When Campbell got up to go he offered to lend Jean some that he had and she did not, realising as he did so that he was assuming they would be spending the evening together. Jean said something about bringing them in to work. Campbell invited her round to his flat and she hesitated.

'Perhaps . . . Maybe we ought to have a night off . . .'

'Oh.'

'It's just . . . I'm not used to being so close to anybody . . . And houses are funny. You have to spend time in them and . . . feed the deep freeze and talk to the plants and that sort of thing.' Jean came nearer and put her arms round him. 'Just things like doing the washing. Very married, very boring, and I still love you and I'll phone you first thing in the morning.'

'I'll be there.'

'All by yourself?'

'All by myself.'

As Campbell walked back through the hospital towards Creech's unit he realised that Jean might have good reasons for not wanting to meet Bones over breakfast, if another early morning visit was what she had had in mind. Only a little later did it occur to him that she seemed to assume that his affair with her involved his being unfaithful to a person or persons unknown. But he wasn't sleeping with anyone else, and didn't even want to, and Jean might, he realised, find that a little daunting.

'David! So glad I caught you. We've got an ideal case for you, all set up and ready. And I'm sorry if I was a little sharp with you this morning. Been under a bit of strain myself lately and of course there's the added responsibility of Rosamund's being away . . . So I'm sorry.'

Campbell glanced at his watch. 'Might be a bit tight for time, Fraser. I don't know if you know the problems we've been having . . .'

'Freeze them, David. Get three or four decent chunks, half a dozen if you want, and freeze them and do them in batches when you've got say, fifty, and you're really confident about the method. And doing the extractions is far easier if you do batches. It really is.'

Campbell, respectful of the general principle of medical science that states that nothing difficult or new should be undertaken on a Friday afternoon, hesitated. 'Is it an IBS patient?'

'Of course, David.'

'Not a volunteer.'

'No.'

'And a biopsy? Is that . . . indicated?'

'Rosamund herself takes biopsies practically every time she takes a peek inside. You know that. And if you send a little bit off to the ordinary path. lab the patient might even benefit. Come on, David. Oh . . . You don't know where we're doing all this stuff? No problem. I'm going down that way myself.'

This time there was no escape. Taking gentlemanly persuasion to its limits, Ratho grasped Campbell lightly by the elbow and turned him so that he was facing the other way down the corridor.

'And I don't think you've met Dr Bophal. You really must. A terribly nice chap. From the Maldives, on a British Council fellowship. Been truly invaluable in the real-time pressure-volume work.'

They were walking along towards the stairs at the quiet end of the corridor, with Ratho prattling on about the Maldives ('Somewhere near India, I believe, but an awfully progressive government . . .'), when a possible difficulty occurred to Campbell.

'Fraser, the biopsy stuff is all locked in the lab . . . I wonder if . . .'

'No problem. I had some sent down from Chronic Diarrhoea Outpatients . . . I'm just trying to remember the patient's name. An odd one . . . Kemp? Kemps . . ? Anyway it's Thomas whatever. And a funny sort of address. It occurred to me he's probably a monk, because his address is St something. I expect he'll be very interesting to talk to.'

They went downstairs and turned along into a dusty corridor, a row of mainly disused laboratories, formerly the domain of a clinical scientist, now retired, who had been obsessed with pus. 'Is he having this sacral nerve thing as well?' Campbell asked.

'I expect so. We're trying to get as many as we can.'

'And what do they actually do?'

'It's only a litle electrode.'

'Where?'

42

'The root of the, um, penis. It's a standard technique, of course.'

'And what about . . .'

'Here we are,' said Ratho, opening a door. 'Abdul? Can I let you look after Dr Campbell? Thanks awfully.' Campbell found himself inside the room. When he looked round, the door was closing again and Ratho had gone.

A patient lay supine, legs bare, hips and knees flexed, head and abdomen covered by green drapes, feet supported in stirrups attached to extensions from the table, in a position not unlike that favoured by most surgeons for the expeditious destruction of haemorrhoids. Between the patient's legs a small oriental male in shirtsleeves sat on a low stool with his back to the door. He had not reacted in any way when the door was opened, and from his posture it was clear that he was working on some piece of equipment, in the region of the patient's groin, which was connected by means of a selection of wires and polythene tubes to an impressive looking multi-screened monitor nearby.

'Siddown please, Dr Kamal. I will be with you in a moment.'

The head bowed closer to the work in hand. There was silence, then a click and, from under the green drapes, a low despairing moan. Glowing lines across three of the monitor screens danced in sympathy. Campbell went closer, looked over the top of the oriental's head and observed, among other things, that Thomas Kemp or Kemps or whatever was a woman.

'Siddown please. One more stimulation only thankyou. I will be with you.'

A similar click, a louder moan and a more emphatic disturbance on the monitors followed.

'And one more to finish.'

'Holy . . . mother . . . of . . . god!' This time the reaction was more of a scream than a moan. The bare legs twitched and strained so that had it not been for the stirrups they might have closed round the stocky brown neck of the man on the stool.

'Now, Dr Kamal,' he said, still so engrossed as perhaps to have been unaware of the unusual assault he had just escaped. 'That is all. I will be with you right away. I must only disconnect.' He stood up, detached various wires and tubes from the patient and then drew from the patient's inner recesses an object like a grotesquely elongated and segmented condom filled with fluid. Dropping it in a bucket on the floor he turned and grinned at Campbell. 'We wash and use again. The patient is now yours.'

Campbell watched as he took off his rubber gloves and rolled

43

down his shirt sleeves. He walked over to the monitoring equipment, pressed a button and extracted a reel of magnetic recording tape, smiled again and said, 'Good afternoon. Goodbye. Thankyou.'

Campbell, now alone with the patient, realised he did not even know what to call her. On top of the monitoring equipment lay a set of case notes. He picked them up. The folder was labelled, in large letters, 'Sr Thomas a Kempis', with 'Letitia Gilhooley' in smaller letters below. Under the heading 'Next of Kin' was entered 'Mother Superior, St Elizabeth's Convent'. That explained a lot, including Ratho's uncertainty abut the patient's identity, the confusion about her gender, her distress about the sacral nerve stimulation test and even her choice of expletive at the last and presumably strongest stimulus.

Still holding the case notes, Campbell went round to the head of the table. The green drape had been folded down, presumably by the patient herself, who lay now with eyes closed and hands together as in prayer.

'Hello.'

'Has he finished?'

'Yes.'

'Thanks be to God.'

'Was it very uncomfortable?'

The nun closed her eyes again. Campbell said, 'I think they're trying to find out a bit more about your condition. It could be of great help . . . they think.'

'That's something,' said the nun without opening her eyes.

Campbell looked round. A trolley had been laid out with the sigmoidoscope and biopsy forceps required to extract the patient's next contribution to the sum of medical knowledge. It occurred to him that he could still forget the whole thing, release his victim and write a letter of resignation to be read by Rosamund on her return. 'Sister . . .'

'Sister Thomas is my name.'

'Sister Thomas . . .'

The door opened and the staff nurse from Rosamund's Chronic Diarrhoea Outpatient clinic came in. Without acknowledging Campbell's presence she marched round to the head of the table, lowered her face to within a few inches of the nun's and said, 'Doctor's just going to put a thing in your botty to have a look and see what the trouble is. Deep breaths and try to think about something nice. You won't feel a thing if you're properly relaxed.'

'Is it . . ?'

'It's a lot less bother than the other thing, so just relax and breathe deeply, Mrs Gilhooley.'

Though it occurred to Campbell that he was still free to desist from the proposed procedure, that might be more difficult now. Good practice dictated that people with chronic diarrhoea should be sigmoidoscoped and probably biopsied too from time to time. Ratho's suggestion of up to half a dozen 'good chunks' was doubtless excessive, but a simple sigmoidoscopy, with possibly one biopsy, was, as the staff nurse had indicated, probably a lot less uncomfortable than the investigation just concluded.

The patient was in good position and her lower bowel was completely clear. Campbell slid the instrument in and took a quick look at the first few inches. Further up, just above a normal looking fold of rectal mucosa, there was a bright red, slightly raised area that was definitely abnormal. Perhaps, as Ratho had suggested, the patient might after all benefit. If she had a small and superficial cancer, which is what the thing looked like, it would be entirely curable at this stage, so Campbell decided to take a biopsy, one only, which might help the patient but would do nothing whatsoever to further knowledge of faecal vitamins, for which normal mucosa was required.

He reached out a hand for the biopsy forceps and slid them through the tube of the sigmoidoscope, checked again to see that he had a good view and good control over the forceps, and snipped a small piece from the centre of the lesion. The patient moved a little as he tugged the specimen free.

'Sorry . . . Almost finished now.'

'Breathe deeply and relax.'

Campbell shook the specimen free of the forceps and into a little bottle of preservative fluid, through which it sank leaving a little trail of blood.

'Just the one?' said the nurse.

'Thank you.'

The patient was released from the stirrups and the table, and helped to her feet by the nurse. Standing up she was somehow smaller than Campbell had imagined. She looked pale and unsteady, so he asked her to sit down and then explained that once he had the results of the test on the sample of bowel he had taken he would get in touch with her again as a bit more treatment might be required. She thanked him and was then taken away by the nurse to get dressed.

Campbell washed his hands and took the specimen bottle with the sample of dubious tissue up to the doctors' room on the female ward, where he filled out the appropriate pathology request form, put it with the bottle in a polythene bag and left it to be collected at the porters' pick-up point near the ward entrance. Unfortunately the case notes seemed to have gone off with the nurse, so that the details on the form were from memory, and no record of the little procedure was made at the time. That could be done later, when the notes turned up again.

Having done, he thought, no harm, and possibly even some good, he went for tea in sister's room, where Bertram and the houseman were discussing the latter's prospects of passing the entrance examination for a society restricted to persons of superior intelligence. Bertram was supportive but not over-optimistic, remarking, when the houseman got up to go, 'And if you fail there's always the masons. You don't have to be stupid to join them, but it probably helps.'

At quarter to five Campbell went home to face an evening without Jean, a prospect that seemed more strange and exceptional than it should have done, considering the brief duration of their relationship so far. He cooked for himself, thinking of her, then tidied up a bit, then started to read a book that Bones had left on his last visit. It was a celebration of the forthcoming two hundredth anniversary of the American Revolution, and distinctly anti-British in tone.

At half past nine Jean rang and asked if she could come round. She did, shortly afterwards, with a bag containing rather more than a toothbrush. They spent the weekend mostly in bed, with a nervous foray out on Saturday afternoon to a beach Jean thought might be quite quiet. It wasn't, and Jean kept her dark glasses on. Campbell wondered how much longer they would go on worrying about things like that.

Two days passed and by Sunday evening Campbell felt that he had been with Jean forever, or at least for a major fraction of his conscious life. Jean was thoughtful, and began to talk about her flat again. Just before she left Andrew rang to say that there had been an unexpected and unwelcome development in relation to the proposed study. As the study was to provide, among other things, a continuing and perhaps highly adaptable pretext for meeting Jean, Campbell expressed appropriate concern. Andrew thought that they ought to meet again soon to discuss it. He would continue to try to get in touch with Jean, who seemed to be away for the weekend.

II

'I suppose I should have known what to expect as soon as I'd got some money together to take a look at medical ethics.' The assistant chaplain's tone was resigned rather than resentful. 'I was more or less waiting for the colleagues down at Calvin to try to muscle in. They're awfully keen on what they call relevance, which means anything other than what they're paid to do. So I was ready for them, but not for this.'

'You don't know anything about him?'

'His name — James Mackenzie, as I said — but very little else. Been working abroad for quite some time, which still counts for a lot down at the college. And the worrying thing is he's got some claims to being a proper academic.'

'What's that got to do with it?' Jean asked.

'Probably nothing,' said Andrew. 'But there is the interview.'

'How did you find out about him?'

Andrew hesitated. 'One hears things. Hammy Hamilton muttered something after a graduation about the encouraging calibre of applicants the post had attracted . . . And I know his secretary quite well.'

'I see. And just the one other chap?'

'Heavens no. A sheaf of loonies as well. Green ink and capital letters, you know the sort of thing, wanting to sort out all those awful doctors. But two other serious candidates. One very serious indeed, as she put it.'

'Local?'

'Probably, from way back. But been out there in East Africa since the decline and fall of the British Empire. There are quite a few like that, sitting in the bush at universities like Makerere, away from the distractions of civilisation and grinding out reams and reams of worthy scholarship. And of course they all want to come home now.'

'Not a medical missionary?'

'That occurred to me too. I don't think so, but I could probably check up.'

Campbell sipped his sherry and wondered what it would be like if the worst came to the worst and he were compelled to conduct his affair with Jean while pretending to assist in the researches of a wizened expatriate in a dog collar and a pith helmet.

'They just can't do that,' said Jean. 'You thought it all up and got the grants from the trusts and all that.'

'Perhaps they can,' said Andrew. 'We'll soon know. Another sherry?'

Jean declined but Campbell didn't. While Andrew was up at the bar Jean said, 'That's awful. What a cheek. After all the work he's done.'

'There might not be anything to worry about. Dickie Dunn's probably fixed the committee.'

'I thought you said he was in Hong Kong?'

'Yes . . .'

'Fixed it before he went away?'

'Hope so.'

'I hope so. Poor Andrew. Even just the suspense. But they can't make us help if we don't want to. Gosh.'

'Difficult.'

'Gosh yes. Oh, David.'

Andrew returned with two more sherries and sat down again.

'How much do we know about the committee?' Campbell asked.

'A bit. Hammy in the chair. A doctor or two. Someone else from Calvin and a nurse, probably Brenda. Something like that, I expect.'

'Institute doctors?'

'I suppose so. People Hammy knows. Probably from the chaplaincy committee.'

'Who's on that?'

'Old Creech. And Bertie MacElwee, strangely enough.'

'Yes . . . Well, Creech wouldn't let them do anything too silly.' As time went by Campbell was becoming tolerant, even appreciative, of the ways of his former chief. 'He's much more sensible than everyone thinks. It'll probably be all right . . . I mean, is this other chap still out there? And will he turn up on Wednesday? I can't see old Creech even shortlisting him, because of the travelling expenses from Mombasa or wherever.'

'He's at Keele,' said Andrew. 'Some sort of sabbatical. How about lunch?'

At lunch Jean slipped her left foot out of her shoe and rested it on Campbell's right ankle. They talked more generally about Andrew's project, as though it were proceeding as intended. Campbell wondered about that, but eventually decided it was quite a sensible thing to do. On balance, it was likely that the chap who had thought the whole thing up and found the money would get the job, and that he and Jean would assist Andrew in something that was beginning to sound more like a series of agreeable dinner parties than anything else. And if things went wrong on Wednesday, and an unsympathetic outsider took over, it was simply the sudden death of a good idea, but he and Jean might go on meeting anyway.

Jean asked Andrew how he was going to make sure people discussed things systematically and didn't just talk in circles. Andrew said, 'Chairmen who aren't doctors', and Jean laughed. 'Lawyers are good value. They're terribly unimpressed by other professions and forever stopping people talking nonsense. So maybe a lawyer for one . . .'

'Death or sex?' Jean asked.

'Oh, death probably.'

At a very early stage of their discussions Campbell had asked what, from the vast and nebulous territory encompassed by the term 'medical ethics', Andrew proposed to look at in detail. The assistant chaplain had shrugged. 'Death and sex, I suppose. Everyone I've talked to says that's where the problems are.'

'And sex?'

'Tricky. Need to think about that. If I'm appointed, of course.'

'I don't think I'll invite you down to my office for coffee today, Dr Campbell.'

'Come up to mine. Or the lab. There's coffee and stuff there.'

'No, thank you.'

'Oh.'

'We've got all evening and night.'

'Have we?'

'Yes. If my husband says he'll be back on Tuesday he'll be back on Tuesday. He's a very reliable husband.'

'Come round. I'll cook.'

'We can both cook. What about your friend Bones?'

'Pretty unreliable, but never ever home on Monday night.'

'Six?'

'Six.'

'See you this evening.'

'See you this evening.'

Campbell and Jean parted at the gates of the Institute, Jean heading for Endocrinology Outpatients, Campbell for the research fellows' room or his laboratory, he wasn't sure which. In the event he went directly to neither, but to the wards, where he checked with

49

the two housemen looking after Rosamund's patients that all was well. As he was leaving the female ward the houseman asked him if he had seen a pathology report addressed to him and marked 'Urgent'. The envelope lay in a wire basket with a sheaf of unfiled reports concerning various of Rosamund's outpatients looked after by Dilys, Bill Dempster and Campbell himself. He opened it and read it on his way back to the research fellows' room.

At first neither the name nor the diagnosis on the report meant much to him. The customary paragraph describing the microscopic structure of the specimen went on a bit about high vascularity, pleomorphic predominantly venular and capillary formations of poorly differentiated endothelial cells and the like. He read it again to confirm that there was no suggestion of malignancy, then looked once more at the top of the report. Gilhooley, he recalled, was the nun who had said 'My name is Sister Thomas'. She did not have cancer.

He stuck the report in his pocket. It could be filed by the clerical staff in due course. Meanwhile it might be courtesy to inform the patient's general practitioner that a suspicious lesion had been biopsied and no evidence of malignancy had been found. Since that meant finding the case notes for such details as the GP's name and address, and since the case notes had last been seen disappearing down the corridor in the hands of the staff nurse from Chronic Diarrhoea Outpatients, the letter would have to wait. Campbell returned to the research fellows' room and the perusal of the paper from Tallahassee.

'Bill around?'

'Haven't seen him. Have you tried haematology?'

'I suppose I could.'

'Or pathology?'

'No.'

'He might have taken a few days leave. Said something about that on Friday, and would I keep an eye on Rosamund's inpatients for him.'

'Tut tut,' said Bertram. 'When the cat's away . . .' He hitched himself up on to the tidy desk by the door and took out his pipe. 'So you're looking after Rosamund's beds.'

'Dilys is on official leave. So yes, I think I am.'

'Any problems?'

'Don't think so.'

'Be glad to help you if there are . . . And the research going all right?'

'As well as can be expected.'

'Anything else in the pipeline?'

'Research?'

'No. Jobs.'

'Nothing yet.'

'But you're looking?'

'Sort of.' Ten minutes with the classified ads in the *BMJ* did not constitute a very systematic search, but was a start. The problem was that Campbell, like most Edinburgh doctors, did not want to leave Edinburgh.

'Anything in particular?'

'Not really. Just not research.'

'What about this thing the chaplain's doing?'

'That's very part time, but interesting. You know. A reason for staying around.'

'What is it anyway?'

'A sort of discussion group, about medical ethics.'

'About not screwing the patients?'

'Seems to be a broader than that.'

'Oh. Things like the size of your brass plate?'

'More sort of ethical stuff. He seems to have started with the sort of things people get anxious about. I think a lot of it's going to be about death and dying.'

'Who else is in it?'

Campbell thought of Jean and said, 'I don't know yet ... There are going to be some interviews on Wednesday.'

'Creech was having a mutter about that over coffee.'

'Was he?' That was good news. Andrew had sounded as if he'd be glad to see Creech, and both Jean and Campbell had worked for him as residents.

'Said something about Dickie Dunn having put him in a difficult position.'

'Oh ... Any details?'

'Sorry. Can't help you there, son. He was just having a general mutter. You know what he's like.'

It was almost time for tea. Bertram sat contentedly amid wreaths of blue smoke. 'Fraser getting you plenty of biopsies?'

'None today. But there was one patient on Friday ...'

Of the dozen or so junior hospital doctors attached to the unit in various research and clinical capacities, Bertram was the most senior and most sensible. He listened as Campbell described what he had seen on Friday afternoon, putting his pipe down and pressing his thighs together when Campbell got to the bit about the electrodes.

'Bloody hell. So that's what he's doing?'

'You didn't know?'

'Well, I sort of knew and I didn't. I mean, Fraser drivels away about how keen young Abdul is, and what good results he's getting from the sacral nerve stimulation test, and you think it's all right because it all sounds very scientific and rational . . . But then when you get down to brass tacks it's wiring nuns up to the mains by the naughty parts . . .'

'I'm not sure Fraser actually knows about the ghastly anatomical details.'

'Not a details man, as you've probably found out. And you can see how having Abdul suits him. Gets the results without him having to actually touch anybody, clocks up the cases at arms length while that little brown bugger does things in the name of science that would be cut from a blue movie on grounds of taste.'

'Would Rosamund know?'

'I doubt it. She just reads about the sacral nerve stimulation test somewhere in the *Journal of Advanced Plagiarism*, and there's nothing about the details. Little Abdul looks up the original paper by Mengele and others in the *Archives of Belsen Studies* or something and goes right ahead because Rosamund told Fraser to tell him to. I mean, he's got his MD thesis to think about.'

'So what can we do?'

'Do?'

'Well. . . Shouldn't someone complain, or something?'

'Who to?'

'Well, Creech, maybe.'

Bertram got up. 'Tricky, with Rosamund away. Maybe when she comes back . . . Have you mentioned it to Fraser?'

'He must know, roughly, already . . .'

'Hm. Difficult . . . I mean Abdul's just doing it, isn't he?'

'What do you mean?'

'Well, he's not *enjoying* it or anything . . .'

'Not especially. No. Didn't seem to be.'

'Tricky one, David . . . How about some tea?'

That evening Campbell cooked beef Stroganoff, which looked more difficult than it was, and Jean brought from her deepfreeze something she called her best posh pudding. Once again they ate together with little touches of formality, perhaps because they had little idea when they would eat together again. After dinner they listened to a Radio Three concert, then went for a short walk in the park. Campbell found himself wanting to talk about what had happened to the nun, and began by telling Jean about the British Council fellowship holder from the Maldives.

Somewhat to Campbell's surprise, Jean had already met him. 'It was after lunch at the Institute, and I was having coffee on the lawn. Fraser Ratho came up with this chap and introduced him and said where he was from and why he was here and all that, and he seemed all right. But then Fraser went away and the man from Mali or wherever started talking about his research and then it got a bit odd. He said he needed normal controls, and quite a few of the doctors on the unit were having it done on them, and would I like to come in some evening.'

'He what?'

'Asked if he could do it on me.'

'What did he say about it . . ? The test.'

'Something about colonic pressures and volumes. It didn't sound very nice. And he smelled of something really odd, like curried fish, so I said I was swotting for membership and it wasn't very convenient. So he said perhaps later, so I said I had fifteen patients coming to the clinic at quarter to two and left him to get on with his coffee.'

Campbell put his arm round Jean and she huddled close to him. 'I don't think anyone really knows what he's doing,' he said to the top of her head. 'He's well worth staying away from. Really.' Jean's arm squeezed him, and they began to walk more quickly. Campbell made a mental note to check around and see if Dr Bhopal had attempted to recruit any other volunteers from among his colleagues.

That night they made love and slept and in the morning before they got up lay with their arms round one another. Jean said, 'We can still see each other, if you want to . . . I want to.' Campbell nodded against her and when she moved on top of him and kissed him there were tears in her eyes.

'About time too, young Campbell. You've been pissing around in shit for long enough,' said Hadden. 'I'm surprised it's taken you so long to see the light at the end of the sigmoidoscope . . . Welcome out into the fresh air. Of course people who've been incarcerated in the large bowel as long as you sometimes take a few days to adapt, but you'll get used to it. What did Rosamund say?'

'I haven't told her yet.'

'Oh. So you haven't actually escaped?'

'No.'

'She might just want you to stay.'

'I don't think that would matter now.'

'It does to her. Looks bad if her junior research bods don't stay and do their time. People mutter about supervision.'

'They can mutter.'

'And there's your future. She could sink you with the wrong sort of reference, or an informal word here and there.'

'I'm not going to ask her for a reference.'

'That might not matter. People might ask her about you anyway. They do that. It keeps the tribe pure.'

'I'll take the risk.'

'You're probably all right. Everybody loathes her. Chap in my year got fed up being kicked round the ward by old Snotty Simpson. One morning he asked for the fifteenth time what sort of school he'd been at, and he told Snotty to get stuffed and just walked off his ward. Word got round and he got three job offers in a week, all from people who'd hated old Simp for years . . . Rosamund's not quite in the same league, but she's getting there.'

Hadden was dispensing career advice over a second pint in the pub opposite the hospital. 'Another thing you ought to ask yourself, young Campbell.'

'What?'

'What happened to the last few bods who did jobs like yours for Rosamund?'

'Elder went off to be a GP after she wrote all his best ideas into a grant application without his name on it.'

'And before him?'

'Bill Dempster. Still around, officially.'

'A right bloody conman. Before him?'

'Kenny Evans.'

'My year. Went mad and became an army psychiatrist. So the world's your oyster, lad. Depart, in the name of god, go. What about Casualty?'

'Hadn't thought about it.'

'Worse things could happen to a young man than learning how to sew up drunks and straighten out old ladies with fractures. You might even live down your previous record and become a useful member of society again.'

'It's a thought.' In his five or so years around the Institute as student and houseman and failed clinical scientist Campbell had always had a vague respect for people who worked in Casualty. It was the front line. You took what came in, unhelped by any preliminary professional assessment. From what he had seen, anything might turn up, from acute schizophrenia to ingrown toenails, and the casualty officer, the man on the spot, had to make some sort of assessment and act on it.

'Three jobs still going for August.'

'Really?' Campbell considered the longeurs of his present appointment, the baroque court politics of an over-staffed and underemployed academic unit, and the rococo futility of the game of science as he knew it.

'You don't have to be brave,' said Hadden. 'You only have to be up to date with your subscription to the Medical Defence Union. And the staff nurses are something else . . . Can I put your name down for one?'

Campbell finished his pint and everything seemed a great deal clearer, on the job front at least. Hadden waxed eloquent about the rich and varied clinical experience available. 'Very little of it's been scraped off the motorway, which is what you're obsessed with when you start. A lot of it's medicine, some of it bloody interesting. Found a woman with hereditary telangiectasia the other day.'

'Oooh, clever.'

'Just about bleeding to death.'

'Really?'

'A very odd story. JG's looking into it. Woman of fifty, obvious hereditary telangiectasia. The usual bright red spidery things, a nice one on her top lip. And some clever bugger had been investigating her for something she probably hasn't got, poking things into her large bowel. So she was dragged in on Monday afternoon, as white as a sheet, BP practically unrecordable, and passing fresh blood per rectum.'

'A nun?'

'Christ, Campbell, two pints and you're telepathic. Yes. And the surgeons took her and she needed about twenty pints before she could hold her pressure up. I heard today they'd fulgurated something in her bum but her kidneys had packed up and she'll be lucky if she's back to light duties with the rosary in a couple of months at the earliest. And this morning a chap from Naples came in from a package tour with a bit of a sore back. Multiple osteolytic secondaries, poor bugger. A case of see Edinburgh and die . . . Another of those?'

'Thanks.'

Hadden went to the bar, leaving Campbell to a gradual realisation of how badly he had managed the unfortunate Sister Thomas à Kempis. Missing the diagnosis was his first mistake. He recalled the nun's face quite easily, complete with the red blotch in the left half of her faint grey moustache: one of the multiple blood vessel abnormalities, internal and external, which characterised the disorder of familial haemorrhagic telangiectasia.

Taking a chunk out of one of these clumps of abnormal vessels was the second. The little trail of blood in the specimen bottle, something he had never seen before, should have alerted him, at least to the extent of prompting him to have another look at the biopsy site. And his third mistake, which had occurred too late in the course of events to have mattered much, was to have read the biopsy report and interpreted it simply as non-malignant. As Campbell thought further about the case, he remembered a fourth mistake, which was not to have written in the case notes, which in turn meant that only a fairly thorough enquiry would establish his involvement in the matter at all.

Hadden stood at the bar still waiting to be served. Campbell searched his pockets and found the biopsy report (having retained it rather than left it with a secretary for filing was yet another transgression, but one that hardly mattered now). In the space marked 'diagnosis' was one word: telangiectasia. He folded the report and pocketed it once more. From the sound of things the nun had bled almost to death, almost certainly because of his unnecessary biopsy.

'Drink this, lad. You'll soon feel better.'

'Thanks.'

Much later, Campbell walked home alone across the park, thinking about the nun and the possible consequences of his mismanagement of her. Hadden's remark about the interest in the case being taken by Mr Gillon, the surgeon in charge of the Casualty Department, was particularly worrying, quite apart from any unnecessary suffering she had undergone. But if enquiries were to be made about what had happened to her on the previous Friday afternoon, the Maldivian research fellow's contribution to the case might well be more apparent than Campbell's; perhaps with salutary results, such as deportation.

It was all very difficult, and as Campbell climbed the stair towards his flat he found himself wishing very much he could discuss the whole ghastly business with Jean, who was presumably now at home in a flat not far off, quite like his own but the other way round, and sipping a chaste matrimonial cocoa while listening to an account of bracing mountain walks and recent advances in Welsh frogs.

Halfway up the stair, with two flights still to go, he heard a telephone ringing high on the right, with the new purring sound that made it almost certainly that of his own flat. He started to run upstairs as fast as an evening's drinking would permit, got to the door with the phone still ringing, fumbled with his keys and charged into the flat leaving the door wide open.

Gasping for breath, he got to the phone while it was still ringing. 'Hello?'

'David?'

'Jean!'

'Hello?'

There was an awkward pause. Campbell stood breathless and aching. It was not Jean. It was not even another familiar voice. It was simply someone who sounded vaguely like Jean at a time when he had very much wanted it to be her.

'Dr Campbell speaking . . .'

'That's awfully formal, David.'

'Who's speaking, please?'

'Anna. Anna Affleck. We used to work together.'

Campbell tried to think of anyone called Anna Affleck, with whom he had formerly worked. 'I'm sorry . . .'

'I was doing my surgical charge nights when you were a houseman up on Ravelston Orr's unit.'

That was somewhat but not very helpful. A small series of final-year student nurses and first-year staff nurses had called him from his bed in the second half of his houseman year. In general he had tried to like them and to get on well with them, if only to reduce the pain of the summons and the probability of unnecessary calls, and some had entered into the spirit of the thing ('Hello, love. It's me again. Not anything to do with the ward, just time you got up...' — That one had not been Anna Affleck.). Campbell, doing his drunk and still quite breathless best, thought of a few more but no bells rang.

'I'm sure you'll remember me when you see me.'

'Oh?'

'We're going to be working together again.'

'Are we ?' The telephone voice was beginning to sound familiar, and the associations conjured up were distinctly mixed.

'I'm still around, doing some post-graduate work, and Andrew Gordon has asked me if I'd like to provide a nursing input to his multi-disciplinary project.'

'Of course.' The only nurse from surgical nights who could have put together a sentence like that was a blonde girl with pale blue eyes, at the time aspiring to the dubious-sounding qualification of Bachelor in Nursing, which was something to do with a local polytechnic. B. Nurse nurses, as they liked to call themselves, were an oddly self-conscious lot who wore brown shoes on duty. They could generally be spotted from the nursing notes in the Kardex, because compared with ordinary Institute nurses they tended to be better at spelling but worse at writing. So far as Campbell could remember, Anna Affleck's record in the matter of night calls had been no worse than average, and she had sometimes made him a hot drink.

'So I was just ringing to wish you luck with the interview tomorrow.'

'Thanks. Same to you.'

There was an awkward pause, then Miss Affleck — Campbell had a number of reasons now for thinking that this was the correct style of address — said, 'How are you getting on . . ? I hear you're doing some post-graduate work too . . .'

'Sort of.'

'Isn't research interesting? And of course what Andrew's doing is really research too . . . I'm really looking forward to that. And the multi-disciplinary situation's quite exciting. I'm sure there's going to be a lot more happening at the inter-professional interface situation in future . . .'

'Yes . . . I'm sure . . .'

'I'm sure it'll all be great fun. See you tomorrow, David, and best of luck.'

'Thanks . . . See you tomorrow . . .' Campbell said that almost automatically because that was what he would have said to Jean, if she had called, and he would have much preferred it to have been Jean. Almost as soon as he had said it he regretted it, because Miss Affleck said, 'That'll be nice . . .' with great warmth of feeling, then 'Bye, David,' with only slightly less.

'Goodbye.'

Alone in the flat, Campbell ate a chunk of cheese, washing it down with a fair-sized whisky, then had a shower and went to bed. When he turned back the downie, which was unusually straight and tidy, he found a little piece of paper with Jean's writing. It said 'I love you' and 'PTO' on one side. On the other it said, 'I've arranged to take most of the afternoon off on Wednesday in case the interviews go on a bit. If they don't perhaps we can see each other (properly). I hope so. XXX. Jean.' Greatly cheered, Campbell got into bed, all by himself, and swapped the pillows round so that he could sleep on his usual side but still have a pillow smelling of Jean.

At eight the next morning Jean rang Campbell, not, as he had at first supposed, to tell him she was coming round at quarter past, but to talk about her husband.

'It's just not like him ... I mean he's never had a headache in his life, apart from maybe a hangover, and hardly any of those. And it's a funny sort of headache, and I'm actually a bit worried about him.'

'He's got it now?'

'No. It comes and goes. Well, he's had it twice. Once up a mountain, and once in the train coming home yesterday.'

'What sort of headache?'

'Pretty bad. He doesn't complain about things unless they're awful. And it lasted about an hour the first time and a bit longer the second.'

'Frontal?'

'Not really ... It sounds sort of ... diffuse. And he felt a bit sick but wasn't, and no visual symptoms.'

'Not migraine?'

'He doesn't think so. He's never had migraine before and it doesn't usually start up in men in their twenties.'

'Not usually. What does he think it is?'

'He's not sure. He sort of thinks sometimes he's imagining it, but knows really that he's not.'

'And you haven't seen him with this one?'

'They only started this weekend ... And I didn't really see very much of him until last night.'

'I wondered maybe if he'd had less serious ones before.'

'No ... David, I know this sounds silly but I've just been doing headaches for membership, and most of them are so awful — ghastly things that kill you like tumours or leave you alive but in a horrible mess like bleeding aneurysms — that I just wanted to talk to you to let me get my sense of proportion back.'

There were two more or less separate lists of things that caused headaches: one that you learned for membership and another that you actually saw patients with, the latter being by far the less dramatic. 'Sounds like something called cluster headaches,' said Campbell. 'They never do anybody any harm. They go away for months at a time, but you usually have more than two, so it might come back, but you shouldn't worry. They go away for months after half a dozen or so.'

'I know,' said Jean. 'I'd thought of that. So had my husband. It's what we both hope it is, but it's nice to have a third opinion from a sensible doctor who's got half of membership already.'

'Where is he now?'

'In the bath. I'm sure he's going to be all right but usually he's so healthy I just don't have to worry about him. Yes. Cluster headaches. He's a bit worried about having a lot more just now, because he doesn't think he could work with one, and he's got a lot to do with his frogs after Cardiff. But I'm sure he's basically all right . . . Thanks, David . . . He's getting out of his bath . . . Did you get my note?'

'Yes. Thanks. Lovely.'

'Good. See you this afternoon.'

'See you this afternoon.'

A little disappointed that Jean was not coming round to see him properly before work, Campbell made himself a cup of coffee, took *The Guardian* from the letterbox and went back to bed for half an hour, then shaved and had a leisurely bath with the vague intention of thinking through one or two of the questions that might reasonably be expected at an interview concerning a medical ethics study.

There was not much to go on. Creech and MacElwee might, according to the best available information, be there. Creech would make a complicated personal statement with a question mark at the end, inviting only simple agreement. MacElwee was widely held to be mad and might ask anything. Hammy, quite possibly the Reverend Professor Hamilton, the smooth University operator, was an unknown quantity, but as such still perhaps a little more predictable than Miss, or more probably Ms, Boylan, the nurse and militant communist lesbian, or possibly militant lesbian communist.

In his best suit, which had got him through finals and might with luck see him through the clinical part of the MRCP too, and his interview tie, a neutral dark green silk that neither invited clubby questions nor aroused tribal antagonisms, Campbell walked across the park well after the rush hour, still wondering about the interview. Although Andrew had told him that no special expertise was expected of him, it seemed a good idea to drop in at the medical library and at least see what the literature looked like.

He made a general inquiry at the desk. 'It's in the basement,' a girl with acne informed him. When he was about to ask her how to get there she snapped, 'There's not much call for it.' Campbell smiled and asked for directions. The girl looked at him suspiciously. 'You're not a member of the public, are you?' He shook his head. Raising her voice a little, she said, 'This library is open only to *bona fide* medical students, doctors and allied health professionals. Do you have any form of identification?' Readers at adjacent desks looked up.

Campbell fumbled in his wallet and found a card which entitled him to use the dining room in the Institute and described him as Dr D G Campbell. The girl smiled sweetly and lowered her voice again. 'I'm sorry, Dr Campbell. It's mainly ethics we have trouble with. That and gynaecology.'

The ethics section was not extensive. There were half a dozen books, all dating from before 1950, and a few loose copies of a journal called *Clinical Ethical Digest* whch was published in Baltimore. Campbell picked up the one on the top of the heap. The first article he looked at was entitled 'Padre to Death Row: Constraints, Restraints, Distraints' and was by someone called Brad Klumpke, Ph.D., Past. D., from North Carolina. Other articles dealt with artificial insemination using terminally ill donors, female circumcision among black muslims and the rights of the aborted foetus.

As it was difficult to imagine being interrogated by Creech and others on such topics in the boardroom of the Institute after lunch, Campbell turned to the books but found them scarcely more helpful. One devoted several pages to a consideration of the propriety or otherwise of two practitioners formerly in partnership dealing with different members of the same family, formerly jointly their patients but now living apart. Another described the protocol for invited consultations in the patient's home. 'The personal physician shall enter the sickroom first, the consultant following but being immediately introduced . . . Withdrawal for consultation is not only expected, it provides an invaluable opportunity for professional discussion and the formulation of a phrase or phrases to characterise untoward aspects of the condition or its management, to the obvious advantage of both parties.'

Even though Campbell had put on a white coat before going for coffee, Bertram was immediately suspicious. 'Come on, Campbell, you're not seriously going to try to convince me you're not trying to do a bunk. Or is it just that everything except the good suit's at the dry cleaners?'

'Oh. That. Yes, an interview of a sort,' said Campbell. 'The thing Creech is on.'

'I get it. The chaplaincy business.' Bertram sat back and eyed Campbell. 'Yes, it's high time you turned over a new leaf.'

'Really?'

'Time you gave up drink, women and research and prepared to spend your declining years being miserable like the rest of us. Basically you need a wife.'

Campbell poured himself a coffee, topped up Bertram's and awaited further advice.

'Thanks, son. And they take your stuff to the dry cleaners as well. Oh. There was somebody else on the phone looking for you. Somebody from Casualty.'

'Hadden?'

'No. Not him . . . Gillon? Yes. The man in charge.'

'Did he say what it was about?'

'Didn't speak to him myself. Staff nurse in charge just asked me if I knew where you were.'

'I suppose I'd better ring him back . . . I was across in the library earlier.'

'Careful, Campbell.'

'What?'

'You're beginning to sound like Bill Dempster.'

After coffee Campbell went down to Chronic Diarrhoea Outpatients to search, casually if possible, for the casenotes of the patient with hereditary telangiectasia. They were not in the secretary's room or lying around at the reception desk. It was likely that, wherever they had been on Monday morning, they had now been retrieved and forwarded to the surgical ward that had taken her over after Hadden had seen her on Monday afternoon.

Walking back to the research fellows' room Campbell admitted to himself that he was quite interested in what sort of progress his unfortunate patient was making. It would be cheering to know, for instance, that she was now unlikely to die. That raised in turn another problem: how to find out where she was now without being seen to show unusual interest in the case.

Fortunately the surgical units of the Institute worked on a strict rota that would have determined the destination of a patient admitted two days previously. Ringing the switchboard, finding out who was on take today on the surgical side and going back two in the rota would take only a moment.

'Wards thirteen and fourteen,' said the operator, sounding as though she had been asked the same silly question six times in the last five minutes.

'Thank you.' Campbell counted back. Wards nine and ten would have been on take on Monday. The consultants on wards nine and ten were MacElwee, Fordyce and Blair, which might prove unfortunate. Although there was only a one in three chance that any given consultant would be in charge of the case, Campbell decided to defer his inquiries, at least until after the interview. No doubt the patient was receiving the best of care and making a steady recovery.

There remained the question of returning Mr Gillon's call. The surgeon in charge of the casualty department was a busy man, and surgeons tended to be busiest in the mornings. Again, there were arguments for leaving things until after lunch, which would in effect mean postponing the telephone call until the following day, as Campbell had already decided to plan his time on the assumption that the interview and related matters were now likely to take up the best part of the afternoon. As Mr Gillon's call was unlikely to have been about anything urgent, Campbell simply made a mental note to ring him back the next day, probably after lunch.

'Anna . . . I don't know if you know David . . .'

Anna Affleck smiled at Campbell then snickered like a horse about to do something dangerous. 'Actually we know each other quite well, Jean. We've worked together for ages, in fact.' She was wearing a pastel pink outfit with square shoulders, lots of pockets and the generally paramilitary appearance often adopted by career nurses off duty. She grinned at Campbell again then turned to Jean. 'How's Jim?' Jean was about to say something but was interrupted. 'Doing some kind of post-graduate work, I believe . . . Must be wonderful to have such a clever husband.'

Jean smiled and said nothing. She and Campbell had been standing quietly at the foot of the Institute's grandest staircase, among the stucco columns and marble busts of unmemorable Victorian physicians, discussing things that might have surprised them. It was still a little before two o'clock, the time at which the three candidates for the posts of part-time research associate in the Edinburgh Health Care Ethics Project had been asked to attend.

There was an awkward silence, then Anna said, 'I hear Brenda

Boylan's on the committee.' Campbell said that he'd heard that too but didn't know much about her. 'There's no need to be scared of her, David, but most people are . . . She's actually a marvellous person. My research supervisor, in fact. And she's published tons of stuff herself.'

'Really?'

'And a book. *Nursology: the Emerging Ethic.*'

'Sounds interesting,' said Jean. 'I haven't heard of it.'

'It was published in Australia.'

'I see.'

'Yes,' said Anna, talking to Jean but looking at Campbell. 'Nursing's really established as a profession there. That's why it's so exciting to have Brenda here, now.'

Campbell recalled Andrew's remarks about academic nurses and asked, with vaguely intentional malice, 'Where does she nurse?'

Anna did her mad-horse noise again. 'Oh, David . . . She's not *that* kind of nurse. I mean, she's in nursing sciences . . . You know. Like a professor, but at the Hume.'

'Oh,' said Jean. 'That poly near Pilton.'

'Miss Affleck? Is Miss Affleck here?' The door of the boardroom had opened and a little man in a shiny grey suit was peering out. Anna straightened up, flipped her handbag under her arm like an RSM's pacing stick and smiled at Campbell again.

'Um . . . Good luck,' he said. She smiled even more widely, said, 'Thanks, David,' then turned and followed the little man into the boardroom. As soon as the door closed Jean had a fit of the giggles.

'Was she like that at school?' Campbell asked.

'Sort of, but she's definitely worse now . . . So I'm going to have to come to all the meetings just to keep an eye on you, Dr Campbell.'

With no very clear idea of how much longer they would have to wait, Campbell and Jean withdrew across the main corridor and sat, not too close together, on a low windowsill. Jean talked a bit more about Anna Affleck. 'Head girl and all that. She used to say things like "Hurry along quietly there, girls, please" to the wee ones, and they all imitated it. I think she really wanted to do medicine but couldn't get the grades and I didn't know her very well but she always treats me like a long lost friend.'

'Same here,' said Campbell. Jean laughed then turned to him and put her hand lightly on his arm. 'David . . . You didn't . . ?'

'God, no. And I really don't know her all that well. She was doing her surgical charge nights when I was houseman.' Campbell wondered for a moment whether to tell Jean about the phone call

64

the previous night, and how he had at first thought it was her, then realised that it might be impolitic to let Jean know that Anna might have reason to suspect etc. It was all more trouble than it was worth and might just make her anxious and hence less accessible. 'She seems very keen on the whole thinking nurse bit now.'

'That might begin to get tiresome, but I suppose Andrew's right.'

'If you're going to have one you might as well have one that understands what's going on?'

'More or less. And she was actually quite a good organiser.'

'I suppose so. You can tell from the bossy pink uniform.'

'It was the handbag that made me realise she was bonkers now,' Jean said with some satisfaction. 'That and the laugh. But I'm still going to come to all the meetings.'

At ten past two Anna came out of the boardroom, aglow with some strange inner excitement. Jean and Campbell stood up and went across towards her.

'They're all awfully nice, David. And they want you next. Everybody's terribly keen on the whole thing. You can tell.'

Campbell straightened his tie and went in. The boardroom, a relic of the Institute's former glory as an independent charity hospital, was a long, panelled room with several south-facing windows and a huge polished table. There were five chairs in a semi-circle at one end, with the committee comfortably settled in, and a single, rather less impressive chair at the end nearest the door. Campbell approached it with caution and awaited further instructions.

'Please, please sit down, Dr Campbell,' said the man in the middle at the other end. 'And we can go straight ahead and get to know each other. So encouraging to see young doctors such as yourself concerned with moral and ethical issues. And I'm sure you know some of us already . . . Dr Creech was speaking highly of you only a moment ago, and I'm sure you'll know Mr MacElwee, the surgeon . . . And Brenda here . . .' He indicated a thickset, cropheaded lady in a lumpy brown smock, '. . . represents the nursing interest and Professor Aithie and I — I'm Hamilton — are, um, batting for Calvin. Good afternoon.'

'Good afternoon.'

'Shall we say ladies first . . ? Brenda?'

'Dr Campbell . . . How significant would you say the multi-disciplinary aspect of the proposed study was?'

Campbell had listened to a sufficient number of broadcast

interviews with great statesmen and thinkers to know the answer to that one. He paused in obvious thought then said, 'Very significant.'

The chairman grinned and nodded. The lumpy smock leaned forward a little. 'I thought you might say that. Now just tell me why.'

This time Campbell's pause for thought was genuine, and perhaps even longer because he was trying to work out who she sounded like. A radio comedy series of long ago sprang to mind. 'Well . . . Different professions . . . different people working in the same place, trying to do the same job, but different bits of it, if you see what I mean . . .'

'Go on,' said the voice of Ron somebody, the halfwitted butt of his sitcom father's humour. Ron Glum.

'. . . don't always get on together, or indeed communicate, as well as they might.'

The chairman's nodding was now qualified as pathological titubation, but Brenda remained grim-faced. 'Because . .?'

'Well . . . Communication problems are more or less bound to arise . . .'

'Because . . ?'

The Ron Glum-plays -Wittgenstein aspect of the interrogation was beginning to affect Campbell's thought processes. To say 'because they can't communicate' might be risky, as indeed might anything more specific.

'Quite,' said the chairman. 'A fascinating line of enquiry, I'm sure we're all agreed. Dr Creech?'

Creech looked mournfully surprised, took off his glasses, polished them and put them on again. 'Dr Campbell . . . I wonder what your views might be on . . . on something that's been a great concern to members of our profession for some time now . . .' There was a long pause, in which Campbell ran through a list of his former chief's known preoccupations. The importance of fresh vegetables in the diet seemed unlikely, but was not to be ruled out. The avoidance of the use of the trade names of drugs qualified similarly for consideration. Parking problems at the Institute, alas, ranked high.

'Communication,' said Creech, to Campbell's mild alarm. Brenda, arms folded, watched with interest. 'Since the latest reorganisation of the Health Service I've had no less than three copies of the same circular asking for suggestions on how to make administration cheaper and more effective. So I've written to tell them that if they have another circular like that in mind one copy would be quite sufficient for me. I could even put it on the unit notice board and that would save them the printing of about twenty of them.'

The chairman was examining the end of his pencil and Brenda was clutching her brow. Although Creech had stopped talking he had not asked a question. Campbell decided to think of a sensible question on a related topic and answer that instead. He said something about the various pressures of reorganisation stimulating a lot of useful and sometimes interdisciplinary discussion. That seemed to go down well with everyone except Creech, who in any case wasn't listening.

MacElwee asked if Campbell found it difficult to tell people they had incurable cancer, then told a long story to show that even after twenty-five years it wasn't easy. The lesser divine, Aithie, asked if interdisciplinary discussion should include clergymen and Campbell avowed there were times when their views were indispensable.

There were more questions, none of them very sensible, then the chairman smiled benignly again. 'One last question, Dr Campbell . . . I take it you would be willing to assist in this project . . . whoever were the principal researcher.'

Campbell had already decided on the answer to that, which was yes for now, and perhaps no later if things went wrong and other opportunities to meet Jean could be arranged. He smiled and nodded.

'Ideal . . .' said the chairman. 'Perhaps you'd like to wait just a little longer, for the committee to consider things, and we'd be grateful if you'd ask Dr Moray to come in right away.'

Campbell smiled round the interviewers and got up to go, noticing for the first time above the door a disconcertingly large photograph of Queen Victoria, or a previous matron of the Institute looking remarkably like her, which must have frowned down upon the whole silly business from somewhere above his head.

Outside Jean and Anna were standing waiting. Campbell said, 'Dr Moray?' Jean winked at him on the side invisible to her colleague from nursing and went in.

'How was it, David?' Anna asked, from closer than was strictly necessary.

'Not bad . . . More or less what I expected.'

'Was Brenda all right?'

'Perfectly charming.'

'Good. She must like you. I hope she's all right with Jean . . .'

67

'Why shouldn't she be?'

'She's got a thing about women doctors. Especially pretty ones.'

'Really?'

'She thinks everyone else gives them too easy a time ... Have you known Jean long?'

'We used to work together.'

'I believe her husband's awfully clever.'

'Is he? I don't think I've met him.'

'They're terribly close and devoted.'

'Really . . . How long have you known Andrew?'

'Who?'

'Andrew. The assistant chaplain.'

'Oh, *Andrew*? Quite a while. He does some teaching at the Hume, with the Honours B. Nurse course. With me.'

Campbell invited her to expand on the subject of these and related responsibilities of hers and switched off. Eventually Jean came out, looking a little shaken by whatever had gone on. Campbell stopped himself putting an arm round her.

'They asked me to wait. Just a few minutes, they said.' Anna stood beside her, oozing sisterly concern.

'Miss Affleck?' The lesser cleric was peering around from behind the door again, Mock Turtle-like. 'Miss Affleck?'

When she had gone in Jean said, 'Brenda Boylan was horrible, but Creech was nice. And MacElwee's off his head. I'm really quite worried about Andrew.'

'Do you think . . .'

'Brenda's out to stir things up, I'm sure. And Creech is hopeless. Nice but so hopeless.'

'It's all a bit of a pantomime,' said Campbell. 'As though they were appointing a vice-chancellor at least. But I suppose it gives the people from Calvin College something to do in the afternoon.'

'And that woman a chance to mess people about.'

The door opened again and Anna Affleck came out, grinning inanely. 'Sorry,' she said. 'Must dash. A tutorial I'm doing for Brenda. See you at the first meeting. And regards to Andrew if you see him.'

'Dr Campbell? Dr Moray?' They followed the shiny grey suit in, and stood together behind the chair and under the portrait of the lady with the funny lace hat. At the other end of the table Professor Hamilton rose to his feet and said, 'Dr Moray, Dr Campbell ... The committee has unanimously decided to offer both of you posts as part time research associates in respect of the Edinburgh Health

Care Ethics Study . . . Do you accept them?'

Campbell said 'Yes' and Jean said 'Yes, thank you.' Professor Hamilton smiled and said, 'We wish you every success in your proposed endeavours.' Campbell, whose mind had already turned to how they were going to spend the rest of the afternoon, nodded and said 'Thank you' in a surprised sort of way and turned to go. As he stood back to let Jean pass he could see she was shaking with the effort of not laughing. Outside, they held each other and giggled for far longer than was discreet.

'Excuse me, please,' said a deep voice. Jean's face registered astonishment rather than embarrassment. Campbell turned and found himself confronted by a portly man of medium height in a lightweight tan suit. 'I wonder if you can confirm that this is the boardroom of the Royal Charitable Institute for the Care of the Indigent Sick.' The man smiled, his teeth set off quite strikingly by his complexion, which was a shiny black. 'I have an interview appointment there for two thirty.'

'Mr . . .?'

'Doctor . . . Doctor James MacKenzie.' The surname was indistinctly pronounced, but to Campbell's surprise the man seemed to be introducing himself as Doctor James MacKenzie.

'MacKenzie?'

'No. *Mm*-Kenzi.' The man laughed. 'M.K.E.N.Z.I. Of course it causes a lot of confusion, especially in Scotland of course. But that is my name. James Mkenzi. You are expecting me?'

'Yes,' said Campbell unconvincingly. 'Sort of.'

'Then you must be Professor Hamilton . . .? Yes?'

Jean was having trouble with giggles again. Campbell explained, 'No . . . He's in there. I expect someone will call you in soon.'

'Excellent. Thank you very much. I am sorry to interrupt you. Please continue.' The African stooped a little to read the inscription on the plinth of the nearest statue. 'Really a most interesting hospital. I am happy to wait.'

Jean and Campbell drew away, not to 'continue' as invited, but as the first step in an undiscussed but agreed retreat to Campbell's flat. Glancing back Campbell saw the little theologian emerge once more, look round, pass the African, who was still deciphering the memorial inscription, and peer anxiously up and down the corridor.

'D'you think Andrew knows he's black?'

'Does it matter?'

'Andrew knowing, or him being black?'

'Him being black.'

'It shouldn't.'

'It might.'

'Prejudice?'

'No. The opposite. I mean Brenda might get very pro-minority. And Andrew said the church people liked people who'd worked in Africa.'

'Even Africans?'

'Maybe. Maybe not. Or they might be so nervous about looking prejudiced they'll just give it to him to be sure.'

'That's what I'd be most afraid of. What about Creech?'

'I don't think it matters much to him either way. And he's so dithery it wouldn't make much difference if it did.'

'And MacElwee?'

'Probably doesn't matter what he thinks either. Brenda and those two from the divinity place will just decide.'

'When will he know?'

'Straight away, I'd have thought, like us.'

'Let's give it an hour and bleep him.'

'Gosh. I hope it's all right.'

Jean and Campbell left the hospital together and walked across the park. As they went upstairs to his flat it occurred to Campbell that only a few days before they would not have done that, or, perhaps more precisely, they would not have done that without worrying a bit about it.

Jean started undressing almost as soon as they were inside the door. Campbell, who could have been persuaded to have a coffee first, nonetheless followed her example. They stood for a moment, naked and facing each other, by the bed. Jean sat down then lay back with her arms beyond her head. Campbell knelt down.

'Come on, David. Just screw me and screw me . . . But that's quite nice.'

They broke for a rest around three, and talked again about the deliberations in the boardroom: the questions they had been asked and how Andrew might now be weathering the strange threat to his project.

'He's probably in there now, with Creech thinking aloud about the parking problem.'

'Or Brenda quizzing him about nursological ethics.'

'Or MacElwee asking him what he thinks is the best way to pass on bad news.'

'I hope not. I mean it's ridiculous. Nice clever Andrew thinks it all up and gets the money, and along comes this chap from wherever

70

he's from, and that Hammy person thanks him for thinking up something that's now attracted some applicants of the highest calibre.'

'What about the people who are supplying the money? Maybe they want Andrew to do it.'

'They probably don't know him very well. He said most of it's from a trust that's mainly in the U.S.'

'That might be bad. They might be like the ministers on the committee. Scared not to give it to the black man.'

'Maybe . . . David, shall I make us some coffee?'

'Yes please.'

They had coffee in bed, and then made love again, more gently, with Jean on top doing nice, relaxed things while Campbell worried off and on about Andrew and the series of mildly intellectual dinner parties he had proposed, which had seemed to promise so much both in the search for new understanding in medical ethics and in the pursuit of his affair with Jean.

No arrangement had been made between Andrew, Jean and Campbell, and for that matter Anna, about getting together after the interviews, because at first they had appeared to be simply a formality and more recently because it had become embarrassingly clear they might not be. By four o'clock it seemed the matter would probably be settled, and knowing seemed preferable to not knowing, whatever had happened, but if Andrew was already aware of what had been decided and was trying to contact either Jean or Campbell at work, he would be trying in vain.

Campbell mentioned this to Jean, who had thought of it for herself. They decided to ring the Institute and try and contact him. The man on the switchboard told Campbell that the assistant chaplain worked part time and usually wasn't around in the afternoons. When Campbell insisted, they bleeped him, and Jean lay with her head on Campbell's chest. They waited a long time then the operator said, 'He doesn't seem to answering his bleep. You could try his extension at the other place.' Jean rang Calvin College. There was no reply from Andrew's extension.

Jean lay down on Campbell's chest again and twined her fingers with his. 'I'm worried, David,' she said against him.

'About Andrew?'

'About lots of things.'

They got up and dressed and walked back to the Institute together through the late-afternoon pedestrian rush hour. Campbell was a little surprised that Jean, whose husband was home again and who

71

knew lots of people who might think things about such a couple walking together in that direction at that time of day, did not seem concerned. He wondered about it, and one of the possible reasons that occurred to him was that perhaps she was being less careful now because she thought their affair might be drawing to an end.

'Jean . . ! David . . !' A male voice, indistinct in the distance, called them from behind. Campbell turned and was relieved to see Andrew, walking quickly to catch up with them. They were well within the Institute's grounds and could have entered them from any direction, which was a lot less thought-provoking to the informed observer than crossing the park together from Marchmont. As Andrew came closer Jean said quietly, 'The black chap's got it.'

'Glad I caught you. Sooner you know the better,' said Andrew. 'I don't think I was too surprised . . . The . . . other chap's been offered the main job.'

'Oh, Andrew.' Jean looked genuinely upset. Andrew smiled. 'They were terribly polite about it, and I think a bit embarrassed too. It was actually Hammy who told me, and from the sound of things the other chap could probably do the thing quite well. And he certainly needs the job a lot more than I do.'

'It's terribly unfair, Andrew. Is it really final?'

'Oh, I think so. I mean, how could it not be? They invited applications and had interviews and they seemed to prefer the other chap. Pretty final.'

'So what's going to happen?'

'He just gets on with it.'

'But he doesn't know anybody. That's important. A reason for not appointing him to a thing like this.' Jean sounded convinced.

'But they have . . . And I think you'll probably both be hearing from Hammy quite soon. You know people.'

'Gosh . . . He picks our brains?'

'And Anna's, if he wants to.' An ambulance nosed down the narrow drive and they moved out of its way. 'It's probably best that I just keep well clear of it. I'm disappointed, naturally, but I really don't think I'm bitter.'

Campbell was impressed. Andrew looked and sounded sincere about that. 'But that committee . . . It wouldn't have existed if you hadn't started the whole thing, on your own, from scratch.'

Andrew smiled. 'I've forgiven the buggers, as a chap I was at college with used to say. I'd arranged to take a week off work anyway to get the group organised, I thought. It's a holiday now.'

72

'Let's have lunch when you come back . . .' Campbell realised that working with Andrew had been another attraction of the study.

'Good idea . . . I'll get in touch. Anyway, thanks for your help, both of you.'

'I still think they've made a horrible mistake, Andrew. Maybe they'll . . .'

'The trouble with committees like that is they take themselves very seriously. It's happened, and the work still needs to be done. So see you in a week . . . And I think I actually do need a holiday.'

'Bye, Andrew. And I am sorry.'

'Thanks, Jean. Bye.'

Jean and Campbell walked on, taking the long way from the gate to the place opposite the Institute's little shop where their ways definitely diverged. Campbell wondered about the consequences of the committee's fourth and most important appointment, and decided that if it had not been for Jean he would probably do as little as possible in connection with the study for a decent interval and then resign. Andrew had recruited him and if they had decided not to employ Andrew he was under only the token obligation he had acquired at the interview.

'We can't not do it,' said Jean suddenly. 'It would look awful. We have to give the other chap a chance, at least to start with. And he literally won't know anybody.'

'I suppose not.'

'And anyway I want to see you . . . It would be so awful if we just stopped.'

'Did they ask you if you'd do it whoever was appointed to Andrew's job?'

'Yes, and I said yes because of you.'

'Same here.'

'So we'll have to meet him.'

'And Anna.'

'I was trying not to think about her, but yes . . . Oh, David.'

'What?'

'It's all more difficult than I thought.'

Campbell said nothing and kept walking because he had a feeling that if he spoke or stopped, their affair might end there and then. Eventually Jean said, 'I seem to be having baths all the time.'

'Really?'

'Yes. It sounds silly, but I really have to try to wash you off, and out. You know, when I go home . . . Home home, I mean.'

Campbell realised he'd been having fewer baths than before,

73

because he liked smelling of Jean, but did not want to alarm her by saying so. They fell silent as Mr Lochhead, the sensible consultant surgeon from Ravelston Orr's unit, passed, nodding to Campbell.

Jean lowered her voice. 'And you think I just want you to screw me, and I do, and it's very nice but I love you as well, and because of that too. So now you know, Dr Campbell. Married women can be very silly. And I love you and I'm coming round to see you properly at quarter past eight prompt tomorrow morning, if I can wait that long. Is that all right?'

'Yes please.'

'I'm always scared you'll say no.'

Campbell went back to the research fellows' room. There was no one else about, so he phoned the Casualty Department and asked to speak to Mr Gillon. A receptionist said he was not in the department at the moment but could be contacted if it was an emergency. Campbell said it wasn't, then, on the spur of the moment, asked if Dr Hadden was around. He was, and about to go off duty. They agreed to meet in the Department in ten minutes and then go for a pint.

It had already occurred to Campbell that Hadden, as one of Mr Gillon's registrar's, might know why his chief wanted to talk to him. An opportunity to find out about that might arise over a drink or two. It was also possible that Hadden would have further information on the perhaps related manner of the nun who had almost exsanguinated, as Campbell had still not plucked up suffcient in the way of courage or indiscretion to have gone to the ward where she might be or to have enquired, perhaps on some pretext relating to the biopsy report, how she was getting on.

In the event they talked of other things, spending an agreeable hour together before being joined by Wilson, the anaesthetist from Campbell's year. His presence precluded the discussion of such delicate subjects, and as Campbell left the pub at around half past six to walk home he made a mental note to pursue both enquiries more actively next day if a suitable opportunity arose.

'I've made kedgeree and a salad. And one of your women phoned.' Bones stood in the kitchen wearing his butcher-striped apron. 'It's ready. In fact I've been waiting for you.'

The bottle of white wine beside the cooker was two thirds empty. 'Sorry,' said Campbell. 'I'd no idea you'd be here.'

'I hadn't either, but I had to come in with a chap who'd tried to kill himself. He had this twelve bore but his arms were too short. Aimed for his heart and shot hell out of his armpit. Quite interesting, really. No end of stuff in there needs joining up. They asked me to stay and assist, and by the time they'd finished it was hardly worth going back to Bavelaw, and the White Tornado owed me a duty so I claimed it . . . Don't you like kedgeree?'

'Who was it who . . .'

'Not one of the usual ones. And sounded as if she was trying to make it sound casual when it wasn't. And didn't leave a number or anything. This chap still might lose his arm but it was great fun. Remember the armpit from anatomy? All that plumbing and wiring and things that join up and then separate again? Well, it's all true. I've seen it. And in anatomy you don't have to dig out half a pound of lead shot just to see what's going on.'

'When?'

'Sixish. And because his arm was blue and cold we took him to the waiting vascular surgeons. Old Jeb tweaked out a goodish chunk of vein from his leg and then did this amazing London Underground operation, with about six anastomoses, and the arm went pink and warm again. Bloody good really, except he sort of went back to the war and you could see he'd much rather have been doing it with a few shells whizzing about and with his tin hat on. But basically a very smooth bit of cutting.'

Campbell reached for a glass. Bones poured him some wine and topped up himself again. 'Is she married or something? Anyway, we're all standing round looking pleased with ourselves and saying good old Jeb then somebody said "Nerves". So then everybody was saying "God, yes, the brachial plexus" and looking at these burnt things waving at each other across the hole. To cut a long story short they eventually got hold of Bill MacMillan, world authority on peripheral nerve injuries and all that, and he came in and took a look and said to Jimmy Lang, "For Christ's sake, Jimmy, get me a Cunningham's Anatomy and a can of lager." Well, anyway. I thought you'd like to know. I suppose what the guy really needed was an armpit transplant. Have some kedgeree.'

Over dinner and afterwards Campbell worried about the anonymous lady caller, most likely to be Jean. To return her call was not a straightforward matter and her scope to ring him again might be limited. In any case she had said she was coming round at eight fifteen and would probably still do so, unless deterred by the possible presence of Bones. If, however, the purpose of her call had been to cancel that arrangement, new complexities sprouted.

Meantime, it was probably best just to wait, and to try to get to the phone before Bones if it rang again.

At nine Bones suggested they go out to the pub. Campbell demurred and Bones, having said quite a lot to the effect that if she loved him she would keep trying so he might as well go out and enjoy himself, went off alone. At half past nine Jean rang again.

'David?'

'Hello.'

'Was that Bones?'

'Yes, but he's gone away now.'

'Back to Bavelaw?'

'No. Out to the pub, but he always goes away first thing in the morning.'

'Good . . . David, I'm quite worried about Jim.'

'What's happened?'

'He had the most awful headache, this afternoon at work. A really awful one. He had to get somebody from work to bring him home. He was just doing his usual experiment — stereotactic stuff in the pineal in his frogs — and it came on again, quicker than before and it was just awful. He said the chap who brought him home thought for a couple of minutes he was . . . going to die, and nearly took him to Casualty, but Jim got better and stopped him and they just came back here. Honestly, David, I'm quite scared.'

'When was it?'

'Mid afternoon. He'd probably been working down a microscope for about six hours . . . He usually misses lunch if it's going well . . . And it took ages to go away. He says he's still got it, a bit anyway.'

'No visual things?'

'No.'

'And no vomiting?'

'No. Nausea, a lot, same as before.'

'Same place?'

'Well, it isn't really any particular place. Just an awful headache.'

'And he's never had it at work before . . .'

'No. It's not one of those occupational things that typists get, I'm sure of that.'

'Sounds vascular.'

'You mean an aneurysm . . .?'

'I was actually thinking of a funny kind of migraine.' Someone, probably Bertram, had told Campbell that uncommon presentations of common things were commoner than uncommon things. Lots of people had migraine, and it could, at a pinch, account for most of the symptoms described. 'He hasn't got neck stiffness or anything?'

'No. We've tested for that about a dozen times. Definitely not.'

'And it's definitely going away . . .'

'Yes, but not completely.'

'Migraine's still the likeliest thing.'

'I know, but he was really ill with it.'

'People can be . . . They can even go . . .' Campbell realised that it would be unhelpful to sketch the more alarming presentations of migraine, which could even mimic a stroke, '. . . very pale and ill, so you think it's something worse. Who took him home? A doctor?'

'No, a physiologist. He couldn't make a diagnosis or anything, but he's a sensible chap, in fact one of Jim's best friends. He took his pulse. Said it was a bit slow at the worst bit. Do you get that with migraine?'

'Don't know. I'd have to look it up.'

'What I'm really worried about is a bleed.'

Campbell had thought of that too. Quite commonly a disastrous cerebral haemorrhage was heralded by a series of increasingly severe headaches, as an abnormal vessel stretched and stretched again prior to bursting.

There was a long pause, then Campbell said, 'He'd probably better see somebody. Does he have a GP?'

'In Aberdeen. Not in Edinburgh. I know it's a bit silly, but we haven't registered down here. We're never ill.'

'The lot at Dewar Road are all right, if you avoid the old chap.'

'Somebody else said that.'

'He should register tomorrow, or even just go along on one of those visitor things you have to sign.'

'You don't think he should just go straight to a neurologist?'

'He could, but he really should be registered with somebody down here. Or the other thing he could do is wait until he gets another one and go to Casualty while he's still got it . . . That might be the best thing.'

'He's completely well in between, and he hates admitting he's ill. So probably yes. When he gets one when I'm around I'll plonk him in the car and take him to Casualty and make them do something. Thanks, David. See you tomorrow . . .'

'Yes . . . Good.'

'I wondered about lunch . . . We really should have lunch.'

'Oh . . . I thought . . .'

'I meant a working lunch. To discuss what we're going to do about

the black man. I'm still coming round in the morning.'
'Good.'
'That doesn't count as work. So see you tomorrow. Twice.'
'See you tomorrow.'

Next morning Bones left early to return to his duties as a surgical SHO at Bavelaw Hospital. Jean came round at eight fifteen as planned. She was cheerful and relaxed and they did not go to work until well after nine. Jim's headache, it seemed, was better now.

They met again at half past twelve, and over a working lunch in the Institute's dining room they decided what to do about Dr Mkenzi. Campbell was to get in touch with him, probably via Professor Hamilton's secretary, to try to arrange a meeting, perhaps over sherry at the club in the early evening soon, to bring together the four researchers now appointed to the Multi Disciplinary Health Care Ethics Study.

After lunch, rather than go to Jean's office for a coffee with plastic milk, they had coffee on the lawn outside the dining room, sitting not too close together on a semi-circular wooden garden seat presented in memory of J G St C MacLaurie, MC FRCS, 1890-1930, Mons, Suvla Bay, Kut al Amara, Poperinghe and the Royal Charitable Institute for the Care of the Indigent Sick, Edinburgh.

In warm sunshine Jean stretched back with her eyes closed. Across the lawn nurses sprawled and chatted in groups, large white and blue clusters against the sun-bleached grass. A little knot of consultants from the medical side stood drinking coffee, uncomfortable in dark suits but well aware that to have taken off their jackets and sat down on the lawn would be to have betrayed their caste quite irretrievably, no matter how much they might have liked to do so. Jean's left hand, eight inches away from Campbell's right, twitched a little the way it sometimes did in bed just before she went to sleep.

'Hello there, Dr Moray. How are things down in Endocrinology . . .? And young Campbell . . . Mind if I join you?'

Jean opened her eyes to find Bill Dempster making himself comfortable on her right. 'Oh, Bill. Hello. How are you?'

'Oh, doing away . . . I seem to be covering for about a dozen people, because nobody working for Creech or Rosamund seems to talk to anybody else before arranging their summer leave.'

As this was, to Campbell's knowledge, the first time Bill Dempster had been seen in the Institute for about a week, his claim to be holding the unit together was unconvincing. 'I suppose Dave here gives me a bit of a hand with Rosamund's in-patients and clinics, when he's not sorting out the faecal vitamins for his Nobel prize. Eh, Dave? Seriously, son, how's it going?'

'Could be worse, I suppose. We've been looking at a new . . .'

'I hear Rosamund was after your blood for missing a research meeting. Something about a presentation? I was going to come to it but there was a meeting of the macrophage group over in pathology. Wednesday afternoon's always difficult but . . .'

Although Jean did not appear to be listening, there were reasons for steering the conversation elsewhere. 'You didn't miss much, Bill. The GLC man might have been quite interesting, I suppose . . . But there aren't any more research seminars now until Rosamund comes back . . .'

Bill glanced around the immediate surroundings of the memorial seat. 'I don't know if you've heard . . . It's not just the Nineteenth International Congress . . .'

'Oh?'

'She's going on somewhere.'

'Really?'

'Saw her tickets. New Zealand. You know. After Hawaii.'

'A holiday?'

'Rosamund? A job. A bit thick, really. After all the stuff we get about long-term commitments to projects that will really lead somewhere . . . She's trying to do a bunk. A chair in Dunedin's come up. She wasn't invited or anything. She just applied, but they're interviewing her. Heard a bit about it at the collegiate members' dinner. So I should think we'll all just be ditched.'

'Will we?' Campbell was greatly cheered at the prospect of so effortless an exit from his research commitments.

'Yes. Tough, really. You, Ratho Dilys, me — but there's an endowment fellowship in pathology that's mine for the asking — and of course all the technicians. And I think the thoracic surgeons are putting in a bid for the lab space.'

'Already?'

'Word gets round.'

'And everybody?'

'Everybody on soft money. Yes, everybody.'

'Even the British Council chap?'

'Wee Bhopal?' Bill hooted with laughter. 'You don't know? I mean don't you go for coffee? He's as good as sacked already. Damn near killed somebody with that bloody pressure-volume kit of his. Banned from the lab for a couple of weeks, till they get things sorted out. Then offski, I should think, or whatever they say in the Maldive Islands.'

Campbell was taken aback. Jean, largely ignored although physically in the middle of the conversation, showed sudden interest.

'Yes,' said Bill. 'A bit of a shock. Especially for Ratho. He's going to have to do his own research now. Not just the IBS stuff. He had wee Abdul conned into doing all his faecal phenylalanine assays as well. Fifty an evening. No wonder the poor bugger smelt funny.'

Jean and Campbell exchanged glances. Bill rubbed his hands together. 'And the best of it is that he was never meant to be doing clinical research at all. He's over here for lab duties only, and he would never have been near that woman that bled to death unless Ratho had put the arm on him. You can imagine it. "Travel's all very well, Abdul, but the important thing when you're abroad is to meet people . . .".'

'Bled to death?'

'Near as dammit, Dave. The word is she's going to make it now, but it was touch and go. Creech is delighted.'

'That she's not going to die?'

Bill laughed again. 'Sorry, Dave . . . You're just not cut out for academic medicine. Creech is delighted because basically it's Rosamund's problem. She's Abdul's supervisor, and Ratho's . . . You should have heard him at coffee. "A great pity she's not around to face the music. . . Naturally I'm doing what I can but there are limits . . . And she does spend a great deal of time away from here . . . There might even be pressure for a review of supervision arrangements, and there would be very little I could do about that . . .".' Bill dipped his biscuit in his coffee then solemnly chewed it. '"All very unfortunate . . . Very unfortunate . . . Particularly if she were to be thinking of moving on . . ."'

Eventually Bill finished his coffee and went away. Jean stretched back again and closed her eyes. 'That unit doesn't seem to have changed much in a year . . . Poor old you.'

'I'm sort of thinking of getting out.'

'You should . . . But stay in Edinburgh.'

'I'm hoping to . . .'

'Please do . . . This morning was lovely.'

'I love my country, but alas, my country does not at the moment love me. It is no joke to be an exile, and to have one's friends shut up in the jails, and to know that if I go back there I will surely join them.

My country is now a land of knocking on the doors at night, a land of men in large cars coming for you without notice and without legality. But it is indeed still a beautiful country. I can say that about it because the régime can take no credit for the scenery or the climate. I miss those things.'

'When did you leave?'

'Just in the nick of time, David. In the nick of time. As an intellectual I was naturally a prime target for them, and the wonder is that they never tried to come for me before. I got the last plane I could have got. The warnings were clear and unequivocal. First my promotion was blocked. Me, with my degrees and my communication skills and my many publications ... They passed me over just like that, in favour of a cousin of mine, a closer relative of the Minister of Education.

'And then there was the question of timetabling. It is difficult enough to try to teach theoretical ethics to the semi-literates they let into the universities these days at nine o'clock on Monday morning. When they forced me to struggle along at four o'clock on Fridays I knew the next step was not far away. They are cunning, gradual people and know very well how to exert maximum pressure on a man. Then there were the notes.'

'Notes?'

'Everywhere ... It is common for students in the newer campuses to pillory idle or unworthy teachers, usually the expatriates amongst us, if you forgive me. But me? And they were everywhere. Considerations of academic freedom have no meaning for these people. Pinpricks, it is true, these foolish allegations, but tantamount to an attack on academic freedom by the authorities, using so-called student dissidents as the cat's paw.'

Dr Mkenzi took a large mouthful of club whisky and resumed his story. 'I was dignified in my silence but the attacks went on, assuming snowstorm proportions, attacking not only my philosophical positions, but also my explicatory approach, never popular with the idler and more unworthy members of the student community. The pressure not only on me but on those students who supported my position increased to intolerable proportions, and gradually the numbers attending my few remaining classes dwindled. The sit-in was the last phase the authorities used of student activation.'

Campbell sat silent, taking the view that it was now Jean's turn to say the few, if any, words necessary to help the narrative along.

'Sit-in?'

'I first suspected something when suddenly one Friday afternoon my theoretical ethics class was packed to the doors, literally to the doors in that there were several students seated actually in the doorway, probably in contravention of the fire regulations, such as they are in tropical campuses. I had spoken for perhaps fifteen minutes, covering the various necessary reviews of my previous lectures and demolishing such empirical and utilitarian positions as required to be demolished.

'I was launching upon an introduction to arguments preliminary to my main theme when first one, then another, student fell backwards with his eyes closed. Naturally I continued, but by quarter to five all of the students, many of whom I had never seen before, had adopted this ridiculous position, so that by the time I finished, a little later than I had intended because of these many unusual circumstances, I was compelled to clamber over a veritable barricade of recumbent forms. Altogether an unprecedented attack on academic freedom as such, and, I am sure, governmentally inspired.'

Dr Mkenzi put down his glass and leant forward. 'Some people are capable of laughing off such essentially juvenile pressures, and I am glad to say I'm one of them. I simply ignored these various academic attacks and they faded after only a week or so.' He lowered his voice and his eyes rolled watchfully round his little audience. 'On the eighteenth of February at two in the morning I was awakened by the slam of a car door. Outside my house was a large car typical of the security bureau, showing no lights whatever. One young man stood waiting and another three were inside. For several minutes nothing happened, then another large car, again without lights and again carrying four young men all wearing dark glasses, came up and stopped alongside the first. One got out of the second car and spoke hurriedly to the man standing by the first, who leapt into his car, as did the one who spoke, then they roared off into the darkened streets.

'A very close call for me, I think. And in a country such as mine one can take no second chance. Next day I packed, and now you see before you a refugee . . . It is the same all over Africa. Independence comes in by the front door, and freedom leaves shortly afterwards by the back door. And always it is the intellectuals who suffer.'

The first meeting of the three research associates and the principal researcher had been arranged for five o'clock. When Campbell arrived a few minutes late, Anna and Dr Mkenzi had been deep in conversation, in the sense that Anna had been listening intently as Mkenzi talked without interruption. As Campbell joined them he had politely gone back to the beginning of his narrative, doing the same again when Jean had arrived a few minutes later. It was well after six before any mention was made of the study for which they had been appointed.

Jean had raised the subject while Dr Mkenzi had been off at the bar for another round of drinks. When he rejoined them it had taken him some time to realise that people wanted to get on with things. His own view tended to be less urgent. 'Of course after all I have been through it will take some time before I can contribute much, but in the meantime I was thinking I ought to prepare some position papers outlining the various presuppositions most commonly encountered in lay discussion of such philosophical constructs as ethics, morals and the like.' When Campbell opened his mouth to speak Dr Mkenzi said, 'It is no problem to me, David . . . No problem at all, and I think people will appreciate it. In the long run it will save a great deal of time for all concerned.'

Anna nodded and picked up her third sherry. 'There's no point in letting a lot of woolly ideas get kicked around when there's a precise terminology at the group's disposal. We have a duty to ourselves to maintain intellectual rigour.' She appeared to mean it, though some of the longer words were giving her trouble.

'I'm going to have to go shortly,' said Jean in a tone of voice that would have done for use with a moderately disturbed psychiatric patient. 'It's all been most interesting . . .' She reached for her drink, a Cinzano and lemonade, and polished off most of it in one. Campbell moved forward in his chair. Dr Mkenzi said something about the value of agreeing on a first draft of the objectives to be addressed by the position papers and Anna too looked as if she might be about to move.

Sooner than Campbell could have hoped, all four were standing up and there was a general move towards the door, in which Anna contrived to drift closer to Campbell. By the time they were on the pavement outside the club she was almost touching him. 'I have my car with me, David, if you'd like a lift round to Marchmont . . .'

Campbell said something about it being a nice evening, and he'd been indoors all day. 'Are you sure, David?' She had her car keys in her hand, and was jingling them like someone rattling a lead to entice a dog out for a walk. Campbell smiled with some determination and said 'Thanks, Anna . . . No, I'd prefer the walk.' She looked at him long and searchingly then turned towards Jean. 'Jean? A lift round to Marchmont?'

'Thanks, Anna, but I'm actually heading the other way . . .'

A long moment of awkwardness ended when Dr Mkenzi said, 'Is this Marchmont to the south? I am heading to the south of the town, to my hotel . . .'

Anna and Mkenzi went off and got into Anna's car, a small second-hand Datsun. As they drove away Anna looked round and saw Jean and Campbell still standing together talking. 'That was close,' said Jean. 'I've been trying to get hold of you since lunchtime . . . Jim's doing an all-night frog.'

III

'When did the pain start?'

The woman smiled. 'I was thinking about that on the way up here . . . And I really don't know. It didn't really start at any particular time . . . Not like an ordinary sore back, with a period or digging in the garden or straining something. I just sort of noticed it was there. If you see what I mean . . . I didn't notice it beginning.'

'When did you notice it was there?'

'A long time ago . . . Before Easter, really, because I sort of thought it would go away over the holidays and it didn't.'

'And it got worse?'

'Again, not really at any particular time. I just found myself thinking it's never been as bad as this before . . . And I still had good days, but usually when I was doing something interesting, or I was busy. I suppose if I had stopped and asked myself if I had a sore back . . . Well, yes . . . But not enough to keep me from doing anything that had to be done.'

'And your weight?'

'Definitely going down . . . I mean look at that.' The patient hooked her index finger under the waistband of her skirt and pulled it three or four inches clear at the front. 'Not that I minded to begin with . . .'

'So how much?'

'Fifteen or twenty pounds, I suppose.'

'Since when?'

'Say Easter . . . About four months.'

'Just no appetite?'

'What do you mean?'

'Well, it wasn't because food was making the pain worse, or anything like that?'

'Just no appetite . . . Eating doesn't affect the pain really . . . And no energy either . . . For months.'

'Sleeping all right?'

'I suppose I would, if it weren't for the pain.'

'Worse at night?'

'Not really. I suppose I notice it more. And it sort of depends on how I'm lying.'

'What makes it worse?'

'You mean how I'm lying?'

'Yes.'

'On my back makes it worse. Definitely.'

'And does any position make it better?'

'Not any position lying down . . . But funnily enough I've noticed leaning forward sort of helps it.'

'Anything happen along with the pain? Sickness? Or feeling sick?'

'It's a sickening pain, but I've never been sick with it, if you see what I mean.'

'Bowels all right?'

'Well, I haven't been eating much . . . But there's something else I thought I was imagining at first . . . A funny colour . . .'

'Paler or darker than usual?'

'Paler. Definitely.'

'Did you know that you're a bit jaundiced?'

'No, but one of the registrars asked me if I was feeling all right. Said I looked a bit off-colour . . .'

'A registrar in psychiatry?'

The woman smiled again. 'They *are* doctors. But he didn't mention jaundice.'

'Doctor Campbell . . .' The receptionist had come in without knocking. 'Someone on the phone at the desk . . .'

'Could I ring them back?'

The receptionist sniffed. 'It's somebody from Casualty, Dr Campbell.'

'Urgent . . ?'

The receptionist smiled and said, 'I'm afraid I wouldn't know, Dr Campbell.'

Campbell turned to the patient again to say 'Excuse me' and was surprised to find that she was looking rather sorry for him. He got up to go, closing the case folder so that the referral letter and his scribbles so far could not be read by the patient without at least some nefarious effort.

On the phone at the desk a female voice not unlike the receptionist's said, 'I have a call for you, Dr Campbell . . . One moment please . . .' There was a pause and an unpromising click.

'Hello?'

'Dr Campbell? John Gillon speaking . . .'

'Oh . . . Good morning.'

'Good morning. Have I called at a bad time?'

'No . . .'

'I don't think we've actually met, but you'll know who I am . . .'

'Yes . . . Yes indeed.'

'I thought it might be useful to have a chat . . .'

'Oh?'

'Yes . . . But I don't want to haul you out of a clinic . . . So perhaps later today?'

'You mean . . . this afternoon?'

'This afternoon would be quite splendid . . . Just come over to the department. I'm usually back by four o'clock . . . Look forward to seeing you then . . . Good morning, Dr Campbell.'

'Good morning.'

When Campbell got back to the consulting room his patient, a social worker in her mid thirties referred by her general practitioner in a four-line letter as '??Atypical ulcer', was leaning forward, still seated, with her elbows on the desk. She looked up when he came in, smiled and said, 'Are you all right . . .' then 'Sorry . . . I'm the patient.'

Smiling, she looked less ill. A previous, healthier person had briefly reappeared: a trim and cheerful woman of the sort seen around hospitals as physiotherapist or OT, or in schools in the physical education department. As Campbell sat down he noticed once more the faint yellowing of the whites of her eyes. He opened the notes again. 'Now . . .'

'Jaundice . . . Have I got hepatitis?'

'Don't think so . . . Going back to the pain . . . Is it tender where the pain is? In your back, or anywhere else?'

'I have sort of noticed . . . if I press hard here . . .' With the tips of the fingers of both hands she pressed centrally just under her ribs, '. . . it hurts my back. Silly, isn't it?'

'I'd better have a look at you . . .' He waved vaguely in the direction of the examination couch.

'How much?'

'Oh, down to your bra and pants . . . There's a blanket there . . . I'll get a nurse to help . . .'

'It's all right.'

Campbell scribbled a few more things in the notes, ending with his provisional diagnosis, a little unusual in patients of this age but the strongest possibility by far, and nothing to do with ulcers.

Lying waiting on the couch, the woman looked vaguely like Jean: the same agreeable width at shoulder and hip, thighs perhaps heavier despite the weight loss, breasts likewise, and Marks and

Sparks bra and pants like Jean and everyone else. He laid his hand where she had pointed with all her fingertips.

'That hurt?'

'No.'

He pressed gently. 'That?'

'A bit.'

'Sorry. I'm going to press again . . . Just tell me where it hurts.' His fingertips rolled over a smooth swelling, not liver, not a ridge of abdominal muscle and not a hernia, high in the abdomen and halfway out under the right ribs: a dilated gall bladder which, with the pain described and jaundice, however faint, made the diagnosis virtually certain.

'Have I got cancer?'

Campbell looked down and met her gaze and found he had hesitated just long enough to make his answer unnecessary. 'I think so . . . Yes. Probably.' The woman closed her eyes and said, 'I thought so too. Pancreas?'

'Yes. Probably.'

'That's what I thought. I looked it up. And put off seeing anybody . . .'

'It . . . wouldn't have helped much.'

'I know. That's what the book said . . . I'm a bit young though.'

'You are a bit young, but . . . Sorry.'

'What happens now?'

'You really ought to come into the ward. For some tests and maybe a surgeon to see you. It could help a bit, with the jaundice.'

'I didn't even know I was jaundiced. Just off-colour, he said. Can I sit up now?'

'Of course.'

'It helps a bit.' The woman sat up on the examination couch and leaned forward and put her arms round her knees. 'I knew,' she said, into her knees. 'But it's still awful to be told . . .' Sitting hunched up on the couch, she began to sob.

'I'm sorry,' said Campbell.

She looked over towards him, her eyes red and wet, and sniffed then said, 'There isn't anything else it could be . . ?'

'Well, that's why you should have the tests . . . But I'm afraid . . . No, not really. It really is the most likely thing.'

'It's all so silly. Me . . ? And it's actually bloody sore most of the time.'

'We should be able to help with that . . .'

'Please . . .'

'I'll ring the ward . . . There are a lot more questions and the houseman will want to examine you again . . . And I'll get the tests organised as soon as I can . . .'

'Can I make a phone call? Well, two. Work and my flatmate.'

'Of course . . .'

'And it would be easier if I went home first . . .'

'No problem. Tomorrow if you want.'

'No. I'm coming in. Because of the pain.'

'I'll ring the ward.'

The woman moved, to sit with her legs, pale and shaved, dangling over the edge of the couch. She shook her head from side to side. 'Sorry. I don't usually cry . . .' She got down carefully from the couch and started to put her clothes on again. Campbell scribbled a bit more in the notes and checked the details on the inside cover. Karen Stevens. DOB 170341. Single. Social Worker. Presb.

With Rosamund away job-hunting, and Bill not around much, Campbell was seeing new cases in the outpatient clinic. An old lady with a hiatus hernia, an insurance clerk with a duodenal ulcer and a teacher with nothing very much wrong with her had presented no particular problems. Miss Stevens, who was not a whole lot older than Campbell himself and who with most of her clothes off looked like Jean, was going to die quite soon and rather horribly, with deep endless pain and jaundice and terrible wasting, and she also had the special misfortune to know what was wrong with her and what would happen.

Campbell looked up as she finished buttoning her blouse. She straightened her skirt and said, 'When I get out I'm going to work as long as I can. Then I'm going home to my parents for as long as I can . . . And . . . I'm not married and I don't have any children. Tidy, really. Which ward?'

'Seventeen.'

'Would four o'clock be all right?'

'Fine.'

At first she had cried and now she was sounding as if she was coming in to have an ingrown toenail done. The tests were a ritual to reassure the doctors. Surgery would hurt a lot and not help very much and she probably knew all of that already. She pushed her hair back and smiled. It occurred to Campbell that she might just conceivably have decided to kill herself. Quite a lot of people with cancer of the pancreas did. He stood up as she left the consulting room.

'Honestly, David, he's bonkers. Thursday's my quiet morning but he doesn't know that. He just marched in and sat down and started talking and practically never stopped.'

'About the study?'

'Yes . . . Well, no. I mean if I had let him go on long enough he would probably have got round to it, but I pushed him out after an hour.'

'Gosh.'

'He did a bit more of his "I love my country but my country does not love me" thing. Well, really just the same again, then he started to explain his PhD.'

Jean had rung Campbell in the research fellows' room, where he had been doing letters from the outpatient clinic, suggesting that they lunch together. They had had breakfast together, but evidently something else had cropped up.

'It's about Haldane.'

'Oh.' Campbell, who had a vague impression that Haldane had had something to do with the founding of the University Officer Training Corps, was surprised.

'Sex and Order in the works of R B Haldane.'

Perhaps it had been some other Haldane. 'Really?'

'Actually it's Eros and Logos, but he translated it for me. And then he started to explain it.'

'In Endocrinology Outpatients?'

'Yes. Starting with Aristotle. And I chucked him out a bit after Aquinas. He's bonkers.'

'He's probably just missing the barricades of recumbent forms he used to lecture about theoretical ethics.'

'Yes. I thought of that. But it doesn't make him any less bonkers, because he came back with a pot plant for me.'

'Gosh.'

'It was at the desk when I came out to meet you. The receptionist must think I'm bonkers too. And a poem. Look.'

Jean handed Campbell a piece of notepaper folded twice. He opened it and read a brief hand-written stanza: 'She dwelt among the Marchmont ways, that down from Bruntsfield lead, a maid who brightens all my days, inspires my every deed.'

'It's not very good. And anyway I'm not a maid.'

'It's Wordsworth, changed a bit.'

'I thought he'd made it up.'

'No, just changed it.'

'Do they have Wordsworth in Africa?'

'Probably for O levels.'

'And he really kept on about Eros and Logos. Who did you say was supposed to have fixed things?'

'Dickie Dunn. But I don't think he's back yet.'

'Maybe when he is he can unfix things.'

Campbell had intended to spend the first half of the afternoon in the research fellows' room looking in more detail at the Tallahassee paper. Twenty minutes further thought on the matter confirmed all his previous conclusions: that it was an important and probably definitive statement from a powerful group on a topic that was of no importance to medical science; that plagiarising its methods to refute its findings would be at best laborious, at worst impossible, and in either case a waste of time; that Rosamund had proposed that particular course of action in a rather desperate attempt to salvage one wasted year at the expense of another; and that D G Campbell MB ChB, MRCP (Part I) had nothing further to offer in the field.

That left quite a lot of time before tea to worry about the meeting with Mr Gillon. From conversation with Hadden and others Campbell knew a little about him. He was one of the dwindling band of gentlemen surgeons who wore good suits and had good manners, did a good bit of private practice and were inclined to go on a bit about declining standards. His administrative responsibilities for the Casualty Department were discharged in the patrician manner, so that it functioned as a service to the unfortunate of the city and as a kind of rough shoot for the training of young medical gentlemen. His 'quiet words' with junior staff were admired and much imitated, the most powerful variant ending with a slap on the shoulder and a firmly emphatic 'Think seriously about general practice, my boy.'

It would be comforting to know that the nun was now doing well, and a more thorough or determined junior hospital doctor than Campbell would probably have gone to some trouble to find out about a thing like that. On the other hand, ignorance of her misfortunes, and curiosity and perhaps even astonishment as they were unfolded, might be regarded as more compatible with innocence or at least misadventure than would a too-interested familiarity with the details, which might be open to interpretation as an admission of guilt.

At tea in the sister's room on the upstairs ward, where Campbell had gone to let the houseman in charge of the female patients know about the woman with cancer of the pancreas due to come in at four o'clock, Ratho was sitting alone. He seemed pleased to see Campbell, and poured him some tea and then passed him the plate of sandwiches.

'The egg ones are awfully good, David.'

'Thanks, Fraser.'

'How are the vitamins coming along?'

Campbell chewed his egg sandwich for more than the polite minimum then said, 'A bit slow just now.'

'Yes . . . I'm sorry we had a bit of a problem . . . which meant we couldn't give you as many specimens as we'd hoped . . . A great pity about the, um, administrative limitations that poor Abdul's up against.'

'Oh,' said Campbell. 'I hadn't heard.'

'Well, between ourselves, David, he's taking a spot of leave . . . And when he comes back he's going to concentrate on the lab side of things. I'm sure he'll do well there. He's awfully impressive . . . Terribly methodical, and works like a . . . Trojan.'

'He seems a decent chap.'

'I just wondered, David . . . knowing how keen you are to be getting on with your biopsy work . . .'

Campbell studied a small vortex in his tea. Ratho put down his cup and leaned towards him as though about to suggest an act of gross indecency, '. . . and with Dr Fyvie coming back in just a couple of weeks now . . . Abdul's going off on leave has created certain problems. For you just as much as for me, as I'm sure you'll be the first to appreciate.'

'I'm sorry, Fraser, I don't follow . . .'

'Well, David . . . What I thought you might rather want to do . . . in these rather special circumstances I thought you might want to . . .' Ratho's eyes flicked up and out, in the general direction of the door, and his expression changed suddenly. '. . . have another sandwich, David . . . Oh. Good afternoon, sir . . . Some tea?'

'Thank you, Dr Ratho . . . No, don't get up . . . I'll get it myself.' Creech looked round the room as though wondering if the furniture had been rearranged since he had last been in it, found the tea, which was where it always was, and poured himself a cup. 'A top-up, Dr Ratho?'

'Oh . . . Yes. Yes, please. Thanks awfully, sir.'

Campbell waited for another glowing report on the egg sandwiches, but instead Ratho reached across him for the biscuit plate and offered it to Creech.

'Thank you. I've just been down at the Board again . . . On a committee for that senior registrar job in cardiology . . .'

'A good field of candidates, sir?'

'No.' There was a respectful silence while Creech dipped his biscuit in his tea and began to eat the wet bit. 'Terrible. In fact I thought at one point Scott Wilson was going to get it . . . Fortunately he interviewed so badly I didn't have to say a thing . . .'

As Ratho listened adoringly for further revelations it occurred to Campbell that Creech was also in a position to reveal exactly what had happened the previous Wednesday afternoon: who had backed Andrew and who had argued for Mkenzi and prevailed; what they had taken into account and how, basically, the committee had got it so wrong. The only problem was that Campbell was not in a position to ask him.

It would still be interesting to know. Andrew would be back from his unexpected holiday soon, and Dickie Dunn would be back from wherever he was soon after that. Perhaps, as Jean had suggested, it would be worth approaching Professor Dunn in a general sort of way, with something along the lines of 'all a bit surprising and we just wondered . . .'. It was perfectly possible to imagine him then having a word with Creech ('Of course these things are all completely confidential, but come on, Henry, spill the beans . . .') and finding out what had happened might just point the way to some development of a more practical nature, along the lines indicated by Jean.

After tea, on the way across to Casualty Department, Campbell resolved that, if the fates were kind to him in the matter of the nun who had almost bled to death, he would take up the cause of truth and justice in the case of the great medical ethics robbery. It was, after all, the least he could do for someone who had done so much, even inadvertantly, to facilitate the recent blossoming of his affair with Jean.

'Do you have an appointment?'

Campbell hesitated. 'Well, yes . . . Mr Gillon asked me to come and see him at four o'clock.'

'Oh? You're Dr Campbell?'

'Yes.'

'Please come with me.'

The formidable office lady eased herself away from her typewriter with some ceremony and led Campbell through a series of rooms to a corridor at the back of the Casualty Department where he had never ventured before. She unlocked a door marked 'Mr J Gillon, Consultant in Charge', ushered Campbell in and said, 'If you'd like to make yourself comfortable, Dr Campbell, Mr Gillon should be back shortly.'

'Thanks.'

Mr Gillon's room was small, half its space being taken up by a large desk covered with correspondence. Campbell sat down and, like a prisoner awaiting interrogation, ran through in his mind various versions of a defence and then, to be on the safe side, a confession too. On the one hand he had biopsied a suspicious lesion as an action quite separate from the meddlesome and perhaps dangerous research intent with which he had commenced the procedure. On the other he had omitted to document this and the perhaps abnormal bleeding in the casenotes at the time.

He had failed to act on the biopsy report, though by the time it had arrived it would have been too late to influence events, and he had stood by while a colleague had taken the rap. That latter sin of omission was slightly complicated by the subsequent revelation that the colleague should not have been there in the first place: a development that opened the way to the agreeable conclusion that the whole ghastly business was all the fault of Fraser Ratho.

By ten past four Mr Gillon had not arrived. Campbell rose to stretch his legs and then took a good look round the office. A glance at the papers lying on the desk discovered no correspondence relevant to the nun's story, no letter demanding that heads should roll or the GMC be informed. That was somewhat but not entirely reassuring; Campbell was aware of the convention among doctors that refrains from committing to paper details about mishaps, cockups and disasters, even those perpetrated by the most junior staff.

Most of the letters on the desk seemed to be job applications, many of them with a smudgy, photocopied curriculum vitae attached. Foreign names and degrees from Basra, Karachi and obscure Indian cities featured prominently. One or two applicants seemed to have higher qualifications and considerable experience in casualty work. In the course of a few minutes Campbell glimpsed another world of medicine, itinerant and uncertain, far from the Anglo-Saxon confidence of a Scottish teaching hospital.

He had just moved clear of the desk and sat down when the door opened and Mr Gillon appeared. He stood up again.

'Campbell? Good afternoon to you. Been here long?'

'Just a few minutes.'

'Sorry to keep you waiting . . . Have a seat . . . Good of you to come over. There's something I thought we perhaps ought to have a chat about. Off the record and strictly between ourselves. And in your interests in the long run. You don't mind?'

'No.'

'You're with Dr Fyvie now, I hear.'

'Yes.'

'Doing some kind of research?'

'Yes.'

'In the large gut?'

'Yes.'

Mr Gillon leant across his desk and lowered his voice. 'I hope you don't mind, but I've been doing a bit of . . . checking up on you. Your research, that kind of thing. And I might as well come straight to the point . . . Strictly speaking, of course, I shouldn't be doing this . . . How do you feel about it?'

'About . . .?'

'Research.'

'It has its moments.'

'If you felt you could live without it, you might want to start here with us at the beginning of August. SHO job. Six months. Damn good experience, whatever you're going to go on to.'

'Oh. I thought . . .'

'If you're absolutely committed to research with Rosamund Fyvie, then that's what you should do. But then again, if you'd like a change . . .'

'Yes thanks.'

'Good. And I mean first August. Might be a bit tight on a month's notice to Dr Fyvie, but if you're sure research is not for you . . .'

Campbell's month's notice to Rosamund would actually work out at a bit less than a fortnight, and end a few days after she came back. It might need some explanation.

'If it would help,' said Dr Gillon, 'I could have a quiet word with Henry Creech . . .'

Five minutes later Campbell made his way back through the department, stopping off in the trolley room to arrange to go for a pint at five with Hadden, who was pleased but not surprised by the sudden development in his junior colleague's career. 'Yes, well done, lad. And it's damn good experience too. See you at five.'

Campbell's first impulse on leaving the Casualty Department was to go down to Endocrinology Outpatients to see Jean and tell her of his amazing with-one-bound-he-was-free-from-the-

95

clutches-of-the-mad-scientist deliverance, but a certain caution prevailed. He had been seen by the receptionist there once or twice too often in the preceding week, and a telephone call might be preferable.

He returned to the research fellows' room. There was no one else around. It looked different already. The afternoon patch of sun seemed larger and brighter than usual, and the reprints on his desk, though still an awesome measure of his various shortcomings in the field of faecal vitamin research, were now no more than so much waste paper. He sat on the desk by the phone, a practice normally greatly resented by its occupant if present, and dialled Jean's number.

When she was there she usually picked it up on the first ring. After six or seven she had not answered. He put the phone down and then dialled her number again, in case he had got it wrong. Again there was no answer. His good news would have to wait.

In the circumstances, he decided, he would risk ringing her at home in the early evening, prepared if necessary to say 'wrong number' in a shaky, old-lady voice that had come in handy once before. And of course it was always possible that Jean would ring him at home later to mention that she might drop in on the way to work the next morning, and he could tell her then.

'Dickie Dunn? Old and bold and still good at his job when he's got time to do it, but he's one of the world's great visiting professors these days. Someone was saying he even visited Edinburgh earlier in the year.'

'I think he's in Hong Kong just now.'

'And quite amusing in a mildly improper professional sort of way. He spoke at our final-year dinner, and had some tale about being naval gynaecologist at Scapa Flow as his contribution to the defeat of the Axis powers. No. It's true. And because they'd never had Wrens up there before, the first lot they sent were all terribly well-behaved . . . daughters of the clergy and the like. So his entire box of Royal Navy Mark Ten gynaecological bits and pieces, speculums and all that, were about five sizes too large.

'They had a depot ship up there, a kind of floating engineering shop that could do anything, rebore your battleship or mend your watch, so he sent one of his speculums across to the chief tiff with a signal saying, four of those, please, about half size. Got a signal back the same day. Four of those half size now completed. Please send Wrens for fitting.' Hadden took a large gulp from his pint. 'That's the trouble with medicine today . . . Hasn't been a decent war for years.'

'He's got something to do with a study I'm vaguely involved with
. . . that's gone off the rails a bit.'

'What kind of study?'

'Something Andrew Gordon thought up and got funds for.
Basically taking a look at medical ethics . . . And while Dickie
Dunn was in Hong Kong a kind of mad committee appointed
somebody else.'

'Where did he get the money from?'

'Some trust in the US that's interested in medical education and
supports things all over the world.'

'Does the trust know that the chap they thought they were
sending the money to didn't get it?'

That was another aspect of the case that might be worth working
on, if necessary by persuading Andrew to be nastier than he seemed
inclined to be. 'I don't know. But Dickie Dunn's department is sort
of sponsoring the study, along with the bunch from Calvin College
who got it wrong while he was away. Bertie MacElwee was on the
committee too.'

'He would get it wrong.'

'And a thinking nurse from the poly in Leith.'

'Well, it's worth a try. Go and see Dickie when he gets back. He
might work something out, and he knows everybody. And like I
said, he's good with the knife.'

Over the next pint Hadden briefed Campbell on the delights of
life in the Casualty Department.

'The point about the folk who come to Casualty is that they
have no idea how to behave. You've spent six years learning all
that stuff from the textbooks they've never heard of, so you have
to sort of start again from the great textbook of life . . . And
some of it's bloody sad. You get wee wifies whose husbands have
been brought in dead with a bloody great coronary telling you
they'd just given them mince for their dinner and maybe it would
never have happened if they'd made a wee bit of boiled fish
instead . . . And you'll be amazed at the number of people who
think it's a walk-in VD clinic. You tell them how to get hold of a
proper pox-doctor, and to rest the affected part the while. And of
course it goes without saying that the sister in charge is off her
head.'

'Hello . . .? Oh. Hello.'

'David . . .'

'I was trying to ring you at your flat. You kept being out.'

'I've been trying to ring you for about twenty minutes and you kept being engaged.'

'Sorry.'

'Can I come round?'

'Please do . . . Have you eaten?'

'See you in ten minutes . . . Not for food.'

'I'll be here.'

Campbell put the phone down, wondering why Jean hadn't checked on whether or not Bones was there, and started on some vague tidying up.

When Jean arrived she rushed in, taking off her coat and kissing Campbell at the same time and looking quite distraught. He followed her into the kitchen and offered her a drink.

'Yes, please. God, what a day. Sorry, David. Maybe a bit more Cinzano than usual.'

'What's wrong?'

'Jim. He phoned me at my clinic from work to say he had another headache coming on and would I pick him up like we'd arranged, and I just bleeped my registrar and told him to finish my thyroid follow-ups and went across to the lab. Thanks.'

She sat down. As she lifted her glass Campbell could see her hand shaking. 'He was lying on a sort of bench thing, and he looked horrible, pale and really ill and he had his hands over his face. They had wanted to get an ambulance for him but he made them wait for me. I tried to stand him up but he could hardly walk so we ended up getting an ambulance anyway and me going with him in it and somebody following in the car. I thought he was going to be sick, and there wasn't anything to be sick into, and the rush hour was beginning and they even put the siren and the blue flashing thing on, they were so worried about him.'

'Where is he now?'

'When we got to Casualty at the Institute they grabbed him and a nurse told me not to be hysterical and to wait and somebody would be along to talk to me soon. You've no idea what it's like. I tried to phone you, just to talk to someone sensible while they were doing whatever they were doing to him. It was a bit after five and you weren't at work or here and . . . It's really silly. I started to worry about you . . .'

'And what . . .'

'A really pompous Casualty chap with a beard came and gave me about half his standard talk to hysterical wives and then recognised me and said, "Are you a doctor too?" It shouldn't make any difference. They shouldn't be pompous to anybody. So then he said he really didn't know what was wrong with Jim, but they'd asked the waiting medical registrar to see him and he would be down soon, and then when *he'd* seen him we went through the oh, you're a doctor too, are you, bit again because the beard hadn't told him, and he didn't seem to have much more idea than the beard had . . . It's really awful being there with someone who's ill . . .'

Jean put down her drink and rested her chin in her cupped hands. 'Unbelievably awful. And everything takes ages. But they finally got themselves organised and decided to admit him for a lumbar puncture and just to keep an eye on him and we've been through all the name, address, religion bit and I hung around until they'd done the LP because they were so bad at everything else that I'd more or less assumed it was going to go wrong. But it was all right.'

'No . . . pressure problems?' In certain circumstances a lumbar puncture was highly dangerous.

'No. He didn't cone or anything. And it was clear. I'm sure they thought he was having a bleed and it would show up nicely in the LP, because then they sort of blamed Jim for not having what they thought he had . . . Not in so many words, but you could see the chap thinking, not what we thought and where do we go from here?'

'How is he now?'

'Lying in awful pyjamas being observed.'

'Where?'

'Sixteen.'

'And the headache?'

'The same. Or maybe a little bit better, but not because of anything they've given him. They act as if they need him to have awful pain to help them make a diagnosis, and the more the better . . . Gosh. Sorry, David. I'm making it sound as if I blame you for everything that place has done.'

Campbell moved to stand behind Jean, with his arms round her shoulders. She took his hands in hers and held them and kissed them. 'Sorry. You're a sensible doctor, and I'm a hysterical wife. I've given them your phone number. Is that all right?'

'No problem.'

'If they keep him in and you throw me out I'll change back to my own and think of some story to explain all that. And I'll ring them in an hour or so to see how things are going. At least it's not a sub-arachnoid bleed. I think that's what we were most worried about. You know, because of being left alive but wrecked as a person.' She

99

squeezed Campbell's hands again then picked up her drink. 'Thanks, Dr Campbell. And how are you?'

'All right. I was having a drink with Hadden earlier.'

'Big chap? Surgeon who knows a lot of medicine?'

'That's him.'

'I met him with you last year, when Theresa was dying. David, have you eaten?'

'Not really . . . I was beginning to think about it when you phoned. A carry out?'

'Good idea.'

'Indian or Chinese?'

'Indian. Anything, but not too hot, with rice, for me.'

When Campbell came back Jean had set the table, warmed some plates and found some chutney he hadn't known about. She was smiling and much more like her usual self. 'Mm. That smells nice. What is it?'

'Lamb korma and rice and the yoghurt stuff.'

'Goody. And I rang the ward again. He's a bit better, and they're not going to do anything else horrible to him tonight. And the nurse sounded kind and sensible so maybe that place isn't so bad after all.'

'Good.'

'And there were a couple of other phone calls for you, Dr Campbell . . .'

'Really?'

Jean started to laugh then said, 'I shouldn't laugh. It could have been . . . shall we say, difficult?'

'Oh?'

'He really is bonkers. It was just after I'd phoned the Institute and I just picked up the phone and said our number by mistake and he said 'Oh. I am very sorry, Jean. I must have dialled the wrong number. Careless of me. But how are you anyway?'

'Mkenzi?'

'Yes. And I could hardly get rid of him.'

'Gosh. Does he ring you at home?'

Jean laughed again. 'He's getting to be a bit of a nuisance. Jim always says I'm out.'

'Gosh.'

'So eventually he rang off and when the phone rang again a couple of minutes later I just let it ring.'

'What did he want to talk about?'

'The usual . . . The first drafts of his position papers. Six or eight of them now, I think, and he thinks it would be a good idea to meet us all separately and go over them in detail . . .'

'Really? First I've heard of it.'

'Lucky you. But he's obviously getting round to you . . . Mm. But not too much for me, David.'

After they had eaten Jean went for a bath while Campbell tidied up. A little after ten she rang the ward again, and was told that her husband was comfortable. In bed Campbell started to tell her about what had happened to his career that afternoon, without going into any unnecessary details about what he had erroneously assumed to be the reason for his summons from Mr Gillon.

'. . . so it looks as if I'm going to have to give Rosamund a month's notice with about four days of it left, and start in Casualty at the beginning of August.'

'Is that all right, David? I know she's pretty horrible and the vitamin stuff's a waste of time . . . But four days?'

Next morning Jean rang the ward early and was told that her husband was as well as could be expected and that the doctors would see him on the morning ward round at about lunch time and probably decide then what they were going to do next and whether they were going to keep him in and if she phoned again in the afternoon there might be more to tell her and they would tell her husband she had phoned.

On the way across to work Campbell was surprised to see Anna's little second-hand Datsun with the unmistakable form of Dr Mkenzi sitting in the passenger seat. The car was some distance away, turning left on to the main road. It seemed unlikely that either Anna or Mkenzi had seen Jean and Campbell together.

Campbell hesitated before mentioning his observation to Jean, but she had seen them too, and pointed them out to him. 'David . . . Look who's being driven through Marchmont by Anna Affleck. Gosh . . . You don't think . . ?'

'I doubt it. No . . . Shouldn't have thought so . . . They were probably just working together all night on a position paper.'

At the gate from the park to the Institute Jean decided to go the long way round to Endocrine Outpatients because it was probably a bad thing for them to be seen together all the time around the hospital when her husband was ill. She said she would phone Campbell after lunch, as soon as she knew what was happening about Jim.

'I'll be in the research fellows' room for most of the afternoon, unless I have to do the clinic Bill's supposed to be doing for Rosamund.'

'Probably early afternoon then. David . . . There was something else. Another phone call last night when you were out. Before James.'

'Who?'

'Don't know. She wanted to talk to you but wouldn't give her name. Am I getting in the way, David?'

'No.'

'I'm probably not good for you.'

Jean stood, concerned and uncertain, as several people Campbell knew walked past. If she was beginning to worry about being seen walking innocently through the hospital with him, she probably ought to be avoiding scenes like these. Campbell shook his head. 'You're marvellous for me.'

'You're awfully good to me, David. I'll phone this afternoon.'

'Bye.'

'Bye. And thanks for looking after me.'

'It's all right.'

'No,' said Bertram. 'I don't remember her.'

'You must. Left just a year ago. Did her second house job here. Edinburgh girl but an Aberdeen degree. And married to this chap who was brought in yesterday. Works in Endocrinology Outpatients.'

'Him?'

'No. Her.'

'Sorry, Bill. When you get to my age housegirls all look the same and you start forgetting their names while they're still working here . . . Oh. *That* Jean Moray. Brownish hair. And blouses. She can't have had any idea what her blouses did to me, or she wouldn't have worn them to work . . . So what's wrong with her husband?'

'That's the point. Nobody knows. Apparently looked like a sub-arachnoid but no blood when they LP'd him. And maybe started with a fit. He's in sixteen and it looks as if they're going to hang on to him for a while, probably because he's the only patient out of fourteen from a night on take who's under eighty.'

'He's a doctor as well, isn't he?'

'More of a neurophysiologist these days,' said Bill. 'I have the occasional game of squash with him . . . He's getting better.'

'No more fits?'

'No. His squash. Bloody nearly beat me last time. But yes, no more fits and he seems to have stabilised. Gerry James was on last night, and was telling me all about it . . . He looked bloody ill when they brought him in apparently, but no localising signs and no blood in his CSF so they're just keeping an eye on him.'

'Who's he under?'

'Monty Burton. Not the consultant I'd choose for myself if I had a sore head, but no worse than some, I suppose.'

Campbell sat quietly with an almost empty coffee-cup while his elders and betters talked medicine.

'They're not very sure if he had a fit or not. Just fell down in the lab,' said Bill.

'If they're not very sure then he didn't have a fit,' said Bertram. 'And if he didn't have a fit then it's migraine. I keep finding people I think are going to die that turn out to have migraine. I remember her. Nice writing. I always remember their writing.'

'Game at five?'

'Sorry, Bill. The wife's macramé night.'

'I've got a court booked . . . Fraser copped out. Oh, well. If anybody's looking for me I'm on my way over to pathology . . . By the way, Dave . . . Did Rosamund mention a Chronic Diarrhoea Outpatients you're down for this afternoon?'

'No.'

'That's funny. Told me she'd set it all up with you before she left. I don't think there are very many, but if you come up against any problems I'll be down in Blood Transfusion, probably till about five o'clock.'

'Thanks, Bill.'

'It's no trouble. Reception usually knows where I am.'

As Bill Dempster left, Bertram settled further into his armchair and filled his pipe. Campbell, who only a few days before might have resented such a ploy, found himself quite calm about it. Chronic Diarrhoea Outpatients was an easy clinic, in which most of the patients booked in did not turn up and those who did rarely required anything done. Most importantly, there were only two more such clinics in the month of July, and on the first of August Campbell would pass beyond reach of even Dempster's formidable talent for delegation.

'Good for you, son,' said Bertram through the first blue curls of smoke. 'I was half expecting you to tell him to fuck off.'

'No point. With any luck it'll be my last.'

'Something turn up then?'

103

'Casualty.'

'Great. A job I always fancied doing myself. Standing there with blood on my white coat saying yes, I think she'll pull through. And getting to go out with that fancy new van, in a fluorescent anorak with "Doctor" on the back. When did that come up?'

'Yesterday.'

'Starting first August?'

'That's right. There's a sort of problem, though . . .'

'Tell your uncle Ronnie. Oh. Rosamund.'

'Yes.'

'Back on the twenty-sixth. I see what you mean, but when you get down to it what does it matter? See Creech.'

'Is he around?'

Bertram picked up a biscuit and did his Creech thing. '"Let me see, now . . . If today's Wednesday I've got five meetings, two of them in London . . . And I don't think I'll even be able to fit in a haircut before the tercentenery of the college. Oh. Thursday, is it . . .?" Did you know that when he was a student they called him the White Rabbit? You can just imagine it. "Bless my paws and whiskers . . . I shall be late for the duchess . . ." Oh. Good morning, sir.'

Campbell turned round to see not Creech but the houseman from the female ward coming in for coffee. Bertram was smiling at his own various jests. 'Come on in, son. Have a seat and let me pour you a coffee.'

The houseman, whose name Campbell seemed temporarily to have forgotten, sat down beside him. 'Dr Campbell . . . There was a patient you said was coming in yesterday afternoon . . . Kathy something. No. Karen Stevens. You didn't mean this afternoon, did you?'

'She didn't come in?'

'Not so far.'

'She was supposed to come in yesterday. I left a note for you about what she was to have.'

'I got that, but she didn't come in. Do you want me to try and get in touch with her, or ring her GP?'

'Thanks, John, if you don't mind.'

'What's wrong with her?'

'Obstructive jaundice. Probably pancreas.'

'Carcinoma?'

'I think so. So just do the basics and then get a surgeon. Mr Lochhead, if you can.'

'Right, Dave. Oh. Thanks, Dr Bertram.'

'Don't mention it . . . I was a houseman myself once.'

After coffee Campbell went along to Creech's secretary to ask about a possible appointment, and was surprised to be shown straight into his office. Creech even seemed quite pleased to see him. 'Come in, Dr Campbell. Take a seat. That one's more comfortable.'

'Thank you, sir.'

Campbell sat down on a fairly uncomfortable seat under an enormous pot plant with holes in its leaves. Creech's office, which he had visited only once or twice before, reminded him again of a small local museum. There were sunny shelves of old-fashioned maroon volumes, a couple of microscopes, odd little pieces of laboratory equipment and various framed photographs, including one of the young Creech in a vaguely imperial linen suit standing under an olive tree said to be associated with Hippocrates of Cos. That picture, in slide form, cropped up at various points in the undergraduate curriculum, each time to illustrate some allusion to the father of medicine. On the last occasion, during a lecture on laxatives in the revision term of the final year, it had even drawn a round of applause.

'That's me on Cos,' said Creech. 'Standing under an olive tree that's supposed to have something to do with Hippocrates . . . Now, what can I do for you?'

Campbell, who had not expected to meet his former chief at such short notice and had therefore not given any thought as to how he was going to start, hesitated.

'Before you begin,' said Creech, 'I thought I might just mention that if you wanted a reference or anything of that sort I would be only too glad to help in any way I can.'

'Thank you, sir. It was actually about something along those sort of lines.'

'Well, had you something in particular in mind? Any sort of move you might be thinking of making?'

In a conscious effort not to sound like Creech any more Campbell said, 'Casualty.'

'Ah . . . Yes . . . Now I think I may have heard something to that effect already . . . I met John Gillon, the consultant in administrative charge down there, at the Pathology Society summer *conversazione* last night . . . and he mentioned that he was thinking of having a word with you about one of the SHO posts. I told him to go right ahead.'

'Thank you, sir.'

'That doesn't bind you to apply for it, of course.'

There was a silence in which Campbell first pondered the devious courtesies just revealed, then noticed on Creech's desk a rather surprising book: a paperback whose cover depicted an unspecified area of probably female flesh marred by an embedded dagger and a trickle of blood.

'I worked in Casualty myself once, you know. It was called Surgical Outpatients Department then. They changed it in 1962. I presume you want to start on the first of August.'

'That's what I wanted to discuss with you, sir. My current appointment actually runs a bit beyond that.'

'But what would you do if you stayed?'

'Well, the experimental side of things has more or less reached an appropriate end-point.'

'And the writing up?'

'That . . . shouldn't take long, sir.'

'Good. So why don't you just tidy up and pop off to Casualty?'

'I think there might be something in my contract about a month's notice, sir.'

'I don't think anyone would want to hold you to that if you wanted to be off.'

'And there's Dr Fyvie to consider . . . As you know she's at the Nineteenth International Conference.'

'Well, if she's not around you come and see me. And that's what you've done.'

'But . . . leaving her unit . . .'

'Oh. Yes . . . That. Maybe a bit tricky. It might conceivably be taken as a reflection on her ability to guide and supervise the work of junior research staff . . . To an extent, I suppose.' Creech swivelled his chair round so that he was looking out of the window. 'But that may soon be a matter of diminishing importance. Locally at least.'

'Oh?' Campbell decided against indicating any knowledge of Rosamund's overseas ambitions.

'Yes . . . There have been one or two high-level discussions very recently, and many people take the view now that in a city of this size . . . three specialist large bowel studies units might be . . . one too many. You should enjoy Casualty, Dr Campbell. My first three cases were an acute glaucoma, a tuberculoma of testis and a wee boy who had swallowed a teaspoon.'

Campbell stood to go and Creech got up and looked out of the window. When he turned round again he seemed to notice the paperback on his desk for the first time. '*The Case of the Punctured Lady*. Oh, yes. I got it to read on the plane to Geneva but I think I've read it before. D'you read these things, Campbell? They're very relaxing.'

'Occasionally, sir.'

'Take it then . . . Good morning.'

'Oh. Thank you, sir. Good morning.'

'One shouldn't be unsympathetic. After all the poor chap's spent most of his life putting up with the peculiar horrors of the world's only presbyterian dictatorship. But while I was on holiday I remembered a chap I know who's at Keele now and made a few enquiries. The political refugee stuff is largely bogus. He was due at Keele for a post-doctoral year anyway, and he arrived about a week early with some vague story about the secret police, which might, when people had heard it three or four times, just might have been something in the way of a student prank. Still, Malawi's loss, and Keele's, is our gain.'

The assistant chaplain, relaxed and slightly weatherbeaten after a week in Arran, did not appear to bear a grudge. He and Campbell were having lunch at the club, not as part of any overt effort to reverse the decision of the appointments committee of the Multi-disciplinary Health Care Ethics Study, but simply because they had lunch together from time to time.

'And I saw Hammy over coffee at Calvin this morning. He had the grace to look slightly sheepish.'

'It's all been very odd,' said Campbell. 'And I've been wondering what the people who are putting up the money for all this think about it.'

'I wondered about that myself. All their previous correspondence was with me, so more for the sake of administrative tidiness than anything else I had a word with Hammy's secretary while he was still at coffee. They haven't been told anything yet.'

'So as far as they're concerned nothing's happened?'

'One shouldn't presume to have views on matters that no longer concern one, but broadly . . . yes.'

'Interesting.'

'And how's the Multi-disciplinary Health Care Ethics Study going?'

'So far it's mainly been position papers, outlining how everybody's getting it wrong. I think we're up to about number twelve. James seems to have been quite busy.'

'And the team's working well together?'

'Seems to be. Jean's had one or two problems . . . Her husband's been ill. But Anna's in her element.'

'Good. She was the one I was most worried about.'

'And how was Arran?'

For most of lunch they talked generally, as they had done before their attempt at the systematic study of medical ethics had begun. Only over coffee did that topic recur, and then only indirectly.

'Andrew . . . Any idea when Dickie Dunn gets back from Hong Kong?'

'Friday. I've dropped him a note to let him know about recent developments, and to thank him for all he'd done to help . . . at an earlier stage.'

'I was thinking about perhaps trying to have a chat with him. One or two people I've spoken to seem to think it wouldn't be a bad idea.'

'I think you'll find him quite approachable.'

'And what about the trust?'

The assistant chaplain paused thoughtfully. 'I shouldn't have thought there's any particular rush about getting in touch with them. Not for the time being at least.'

'This will feel cold and a bit uncomfortable but it shouldn't hurt and you're to tell me if it does.'

'Right, doc.'

'Take some deep breaths and you'll probably find that helps you to relax. And you'll probably feel a little uncomfortable and distended as I pump a little air in . . . Good. That's it. Thank you. A little more relaxed if you can. Good.'

The man was more co-operative than average, and Campbell had had a good look up to about twenty centimetres when the phone rang. For a variety of reasons the procedure was not one which could be abandoned halfway through. The phone continued to ring as Campbell eased the instrument gradually back to the outside world, looking round again as one was supposed to do, but perhaps a little more quickly.

'Now a little more discomfort and that's it finished.' Campbell reached for the obturator which rendered the last moments of the procedure less uncomfortable, slotted it down the tube and withdrew the sigmoidoscope. The phone stopped ringing.

'Everything seems all right, Mr Garvin. I hope it wasn't too uncomfortable.'

'My forty-fourth. You're not the worst.'

'If you'd like to get your things on again and make an appointment at the desk for another three months from now . . .' As the man dressed Campbell scribbled the date and four or five words remarkably similar to the page and a half of regular three monthly scribbles above them in the case notes.

'Cheers, doc. See you in three months.'

'Goodbye, Mr Garvin.'

Campbell had started to dial Jean's extension before the man was fully out of the door. It rang and rang again and she did not answer it. The clinic nurse, an angular middle-aged woman who always looked as though she was wearing someone else's false teeth, came in with a large bundle of case notes, dumped them on the desk and grinned. 'Busy for July, isn't it, Dr Campbell?'

'You've got a new woman, haven't you. A tidy one. Not that I mind, in fact it's quite nice to come home to a clean kitchen. It's just I like to know what's going on. Oh, and one of the old ones phoned, just about ten minutes ago. Sounded quite upset but wouldn't leave her name or phone number.'

'What?'

'The one that just phoned. She wasn't the one from a few days ago and she sounded upset. So she's one of the old ones. Stands to reason.'

'How's Bavelaw?'

'It's funny. I've just worked it out. It's like an air station from a forties movie, without the runways. Miles from anywhere and just rows of huts and a lot of wet grass, and people putting up with it because there's a war on. But the cutting's all right. And the armpit's doing really well. Saw him this afternoon. Just about moving one finger. We'll present him at grand rounds if it really does move. Pub?'

'I've just got to make a phone call.'

'Go right ahead. I won't listen.'

Campbell closed the door anyway. There was no reply from Jean's home number. There had been no reply from her extension in the hospital all afternoon. The likeliest thing was that she was visiting her sick husband, who would almost certainly, from what Bill had said that morning over coffee, be staying in ward sixteen for a few more days at least, even if he only had migraine.

On the way downstairs Campbell enquired as tactfully as possible whether Bones was planning to go, as he sometimes did, back to

Bavelaw that night. Bones was non-committal, which rather complicated Campbell's own plans for the evening, but the immediate problem remained that of contacting Jean.

On the way over to the pub Campbell told Bones about his imminent move to Casualty. Bones was enthusiastic. 'It's a proper job, on the National Health, not mucking about in silly research. And even if you still want to be a physician you'll at least get to see the sort of things surgeons are up against. But basically it means when people ask me what you're doing these days I won't have to sound as if I'm making excuses for you.'

'He's been lying flat on his back most of today, because of the LP. And he's still got a headache, either because of the LP or his own headache taking a longer time to go away. And he just . . . looks ill.'

'And the LP?'

'No blood. You knew that. But a slightly worrying thing. The protein's just the upper limit of normal. And they're muttering about that being all right, because he probably had a fit and you get that after fits. But he didn't have a fit. His friend Archie saw everything that happened, and he knows what a fit looks like, and he didn't have one.'

'So what do they think . . .' The phone made the sound for more money, and Campbell delved in his pockets with his free hand, finding a coin just in time.

'Good. You're still there . . . Honestly, David, I'm fed up with them. They won't really tell me anything, and half the time I think it's because they know it's something pretty nasty, or at least suspect it, and the other half because they haven't a clue but won't admit it . . . Where are you, David?'

'A payphone near the Institute . . . I've been trying to ring you off and on since lunchtime.'

'Gosh, sorry, David . . . And I can't really come and see you tonight . . . It's all getting a bit complicated with parents and things . . .'

'Yes, I suppose . . .'

'Come round and see me, David.'

'What about the parents and things?'

'Oh, they're just on the phone . . . But they know my real number.'

'Well, I could let you get them all sorted out and come round.'

'Any time, David. But the sooner the better because I'm cooking for us and I didn't have time for any lunch.'

'Thanks, Jean. See you soon.'

Campbell rejoined Bones and Wilson, the anaesthetist, who was in the middle of a complicated story about the shortcomings of the Institute's disaster plan, as recently exposed by an exercise simulating the collapse of the Scott monument on top of several double-decker buses. When Campbell finished his drink and excused himself Bones was scornful. 'She may be a wonderful fuck, Campbell, but soon you'll have to know all this stuff. The next time it happens it could be for real, with you on by yourself in Casualty in the middle of the night . . . Then you'll be sorry. And does that mean it's all right for me to stay in my own flat tonight . . ? Gee, thanks.'

Jean came to the door with her finger to her lips. 'I'm on the phone. You'll just have to be the Jehovah's witnesses. I shouldn't be long.' She directed him into the kitchen, where there was a nice smell of something Italian, and went back to the phone.

'Sorry . . . No, it's all right . . . Yes. They always keep people in after that test, whatever it shows . . . Much better . . . Well, I probably will if there's nothing definite from the registrar chap tomorrow . . . I don't know, but I think they will . . . No, he's too young for that . . . Yes, I'll tell him . . . Thanks, mum. No. I'm all right. Don't worry . . . Bye.'

Jean came into the kitchen smiling but looking as though she could do with a drink. 'I think that's them all. God, I hope it is. Mmm, David. Glad you came so quickly. I'm starving.'

'Is there anything I can help with?'

'I think everything's done except the table. Plates over there, most of the rest in there, and I'll have another worry about my spaghetti. How are you?'

'Fine. Still high on getting out of faecal vitamins. And I had lunch with Andrew.'

'How's he . . ? Still fed up.'

'I don't think so . . . Very sane about everything.'

'James is getting worse. Another poem today . . . and I ran into Anna bustling around doing her silly research. She thinks he's wonderful. "Genuinely intellectual, and such a fresh perspective on things. He's really got me thinking again . . .".'

'Hm. That as well . . .'

'David. They might not be . . . There's a bottle of fairly awful red plonk somewhere. There.'

Campbell opened it and they drank a cheerful, undefined toast,

111

then ate Jean's spaghetti bolognese and a salad. There was only one further phone call that evening, from James Mkenzi. Jean handled it with a firmness, even abruptness, that surprised Campbell.

No more relatives called, and there was no news or urgent summons from the hospital that night. Campbell slept badly, in a room that was the wrong way round, on a bed softer than his own, with blankets rather than a downie, a loudly ticking alarm clock on the bedside table and Jean on the wrong side. Jean, as always, slept well.

On the way to work the next morning they talked again about what Jean continued to call 'Andrew's study'. As Campbell had still not had an opportunity to discuss any of the steadily increasing number of position papers with their author, he could not contribute much, but Jean had been unimpressed.

'Surely the point of the whole thing was to get people who actually make decisions about difficult things to talk about how they make them with people who can understand what they're talking about. And it would have been fun. All that man's done so far is written out a lot of boring things from books and bored people to death with them. Honestly, he just talks, and his idea of a discussion is saying things he thinks you would say if you could be bothered listening to him and then explaining why you would be wrong.

'"Now you might say, Jean, that surely the ultimate determinant of a decision of that nature is empirical, but that would take us no further forward, because you are simply describing what you do, not why you do it, and I have already demonstrated the circularity of proceeding in that way . . . If I might explain again briefly . . ." That's what he *always* says, but he never does it. No. That's not true. Sometimes he says, "If I might briefly explain again."'

'Poor old you.'

'Yes . . . And I might even begin to feel sorry for Anna.'

They walked in silence, and Campbell contemplated his minor good fortune in hitherto avoiding any prolonged exposure to Dr Mkenzi in person, on paper or on the telephone. Jean, who had had to put up with much more, might not do so indefinitely. The original intention, which had been to advance a number of causes, including that of the painless study of medical ethics by a series of mildly intellectual dinner parties, now seemed sadly and hopelessly remote.

'So what are we going to do, Dr Campbell?'

'I've been wondering about that.'

'I don't know this Dunn person.'

'I sort- of know who he is, and I've found out a bit about him. Hadden makes him sound fairly tough and wily, and Andrew says he's approachable. So I think I'll approach him, when he gets back.'

'When's that?'

'Friday.'

'Good.'

'And Andrew says the trust doesn't know anything about the funny committee yet.'

'That's nice. And this Dunn chap is keen on Andrew doing the study?'

'I suppose so. He must have been. Andrew wanted him as a kind of godfather for it, and he agreed.'

'And he went away, and things went wrong.'

'More or less.'

'Well, when he gets back he can sort things out.'

With his career in clinical research now drawing peacefully towards its close, Campbell had decided to prepare a report for Dr Fyvie, his supervisor, basing it on the outline of his proposed presentation to her research symposium. The circumstances now prevailing permitted a more factual approach and his first and final draft, free from self-justification, methodological prevarication and the customary fastidiously cautious optimism, came out at just under three hundred words.

He took it along to the typist's office and returned to the research fellows' room to start clearing his desk. Among the drafts, results, reprints and unopened *BMJs* he found a small envelope addressed to Dr Campbell, c/o Dr Fyvie's Outpatient Clinic, RCI. It contained a folded card decorated with a Mabel Lucy Atwell drawing of a little girl with big feet. There was no printed message, only a scribbled 'Thanks for your help' and a not immediately legible signature, possibly of a Kay somebody. Gratitude expressed in writing being unusual but not unknown in the NHS, he was about to pocket it without further thought when he noticed a scribble on the back which deciphered, puzzlingly, to 'I tried to phone'. It did not mean much.

Later in the morning, over coffee in the upstairs ward sister's room, when the houseman again reported that the expected female admission for pancreatic investigations had not arrived, he realised who it was from. Karen Stevens, the social worker, was grateful for his assessment but clearly had doubts about the benefits of further involvement with hospitals at this stage. Perhaps another note would follow.

As Bill Dempster had predicted, Jean's husband stayed in ward sixteen. Jean remained unimpressed. Later in the week, after dinner, she reported on his progress.

'They've put him in a single room because he's a doctor, and because he's in a single room they seem to forget all about him for most of the time. And he's still having headaches, and when they remember him they just think of something else silly he might have, and start another lot of tests — brucellosis was today's bright idea — and of course it'll be ages before they're really sure he's not got brucellosis so they'll think of a few other silly things he hasn't got to pass the time and show that they know lots more causes of a sore head.'

'How is he?'

'Getting a bit fed up, but because he's a doctor he's got to try extra hard to be a good patient, and not complain or have ideas of his own.'

'And the headaches?'

'That's the worrying bit. They used to go away completely in between, but now . . . Well, he says he's got a sort of a headache, not awful but definitely there, practically all of the time. And that makes me think there might be something quite seriously wrong.'

'But nothing's shown up yet . . .'

'I got hold of the chap who seems to know most about it, a Dr Swift, and really pushed him to tell me what they had that was definitely abnormal . . . And when it comes down to it there's really nothing, apart from the slightly, probably just upper limit of normal protein from the LP. And he said they were probably going to repeat it fairly soon and see if it had changed. Then he started a line he hadn't tried before, and quite nasty.'

'What?'

'Basically, has he really got a headache or does he just think he's got a headache? Does he enjoy his work? Does he like squinting down a dissecting microscope all day and sometimes all night? Does he normally worry a lot about his health? And does he have any particular worries just now? That sort of thing. Really nasty. But silly as well as nasty, because if he says he's got a headache then he's got a headache, he's not neurotic, and he's not the worrying type . . . Sorry.'

'Why sorry?'

'Because it must be very boring for you, listening to me go on and on about hospitals and headaches. Let's go to bed.'

'And so I think you will understand, David, my reasons for thinking that as we are to be working together I consider it important for me to understand *how* you work, as well as where you work and what you work at. And as I become familiar with what little has been written about medical ethics *per se* I find myself very much attracted to the American idea of the hospital philosopher, which is coming in to the more advanced schools of the West Coast, and will, I expect, like the hamburger and the jet plane, cross the Atlantic and soon become commonplace in the British Isles. For my part I certainly hope so, as I am sure there is a great contribution to be made.'

'But what do they do?'

'As I understand it, they primarily offer a consultative service in the difficult cases, providing a theoretical background for the discussions . . . These are the relevant utilitarian arguments, that kind of thing . . . And of course with the experience of abstract discussion far in advance of most medical clinicians, not only a framework but standards can be provided. It was a most interesting piece of work, in the *Clinical Ethical Digest* only last month, by a philosopher clinician, and I propose to summarise and annotate the arguments presented and circulate them to my research staff fairly soon.'

'I'm not sure . . .'

'You might of course argue that the concept is an unfamiliar one, but any philosopher worth his salt will tell you that that is not an argument. Antiseptics themselves were at one time unfamiliar, if you perceive the analogy. And I think that is why I am so much in favour of the inter-disciplinary aspect of the study we are now undertaking. Medicine has so much to learn from philosophy.'

'I think originally the idea . . .'

'Yes. Of course, David. I am also taking into account the contribution of the nurse, and by that I mean not only the academic nurse but also the working nurse from the ward-level situation . . .'

It seemed that Dr Mkenzi had been making the most of time spent with Miss Affleck, which was interesting in its way. Campbell ceased to listen and began to think of how to get him out of the research fellows' room, not only because it would be embarrassing if someone else came in to work there, but because he had been there for three quarters of an hour and Campbell was feeling a more than ordinary need for his morning coffee. And after that, he decided, he was going to go straight over to the Department of Obstetrics and Gynaecology to try to arrange an appointment to see Dickie Dunn.

'. . . possible to envisage how argument might sweep back and forth over a field of reasoning and debate defined in its outer limits

115

by the three poles of reference, Eros, Thanatos and Logos, a conceptualisation I think you will find both illuminating and at the same time unifying, David, as we proceed. For these are our terms of reference, and as a group we are well equipped to chart the territory together. Did you know, for example, that it now seems highly likely that the unfortunate other James, the husband of Jean, is going to die soon of a cancer of the brain?'

Mkenzi paused, as though expecting to be congratulated on his rapid mastery of local happenings. Miss Affleck sprang again to mind, but Campbell said nothing and continued to listen. Mkenzi, perhaps relieved after all not to have been interrupted, took a deep breath and carried on.

'So I think this will effectively prevent us from discussing the problems of death, or Thanatos, in a fashion too abstract for our colleagues.'

'But you can't . . .'

'You will observe, David, that I have already recognised the preference of medically conditioned people for an almost infantile concreteness of thought, but in these circumstances it might be possible by skilful steering of discussion between the Scylla of example and the Charybdis of abstraction to turn the misfortune, indeed tragedy, to our collective and permanent advantage as investigators.'

'As far as I know Jean's husband hasn't . . .'

Dr Mkenzi smiled patiently. 'I think our psychoanalytic friends would perhaps call that attitude denial, David, but there is no doubt that it exists and looms large in lay thinking around the Thanatos pole of our far-ranging discussions. I will certainly make a note of it. I am grateful to you for bringing it once more to my attention.'

The door of the research fellows' room opened a little. Campbell said 'Yes?' loudly and one of the housemen came in, diffident in the unexpected presence of Mkenzi but evidently in search of Campbell, who got up and went across towards him.

'Dr Campbell, that female admission you had arranged turned up . . .'

'Ah. Thank you, John . . . Dr Mkenzi, I'm afraid something rather urgent . . .'

Mkenzi rose to his feet and for an interesting moment Campbell wondered if the concept of the hospital philosopher would require to be resisted with physical violence. The houseman looked from Mkenzi to Campbell. 'It's not . . .'

'I know,' said Campbell. 'Not something that can wait. . . I'm on my way. Please excuse me, Dr Mkenzi. And just send me all the papers, please . . . Goodbye. Thank you.'

Campbell hustled the houseman from the room and marched him along the corridor towards the ward. Mkenzi did not follow.

'It really isn't urgent, Dr Campbell . . . and she hasn't come in to us. It's just I thought you'd like to know she was admitted to the female ward on take last night but they couldn't do much for her. Some sort of overdose, they thought. Probably alcohol and Distalgesic.'

'Dr Campbell? And I think we've met before.'

Waiting in the corridor outside Professor Dunn's office, Campbell had been cheered by a sudden recollection of having waited there on a previous occasion. As a very junior medical student he had applied for a year's leave of absence from the course, and been told that to get it he would have to be interviewed by a remote dignitary then acting as pre-clinical dean, and convince him of the validity of his reasons for so eccentric a request, and probably of his mental health as well.

The interview had been remarkably brief. The most senior medical figure Campbell had yet met had not even asked him to sit down. 'What's all this, Campbell?'

'I'd like a year off to go on a sort of volunteer thing in the third world, sir.'

'No one's ever asked for that before.'

'Oh, well . . .'

'But that's not a reason for stopping you. Enjoy yourself. Good morning. Details to my secretary outside.'

On this occasion Campbell was asked to sit down.

'You've asked to see me about the Health Care Ethics Study, I believe.'

'Yessir.'

'What's the problem?'

'I wondered if you'd heard, sir, about the, um, appointment committee.'

'Yes.'

'It now appears that there might be . . . some problems that perhaps hadn't been foreseen.'

'Not as I understand it.'

'Well, when the committee met and appointed . . .'

'Yes. Professor Hamilton's told me all about it. Good field of candidates. Junior people happy to serve under best man

117

interviewed. No problems. The chap's started, I hear.'

'Yessir.'

'Splendid. So you'll all get on with it.'

It was an order, not a request, still less a plea to make allowances for a committee the speaker had unavoidably failed to attend.

'Good of you to come along anyway, Campbell.'

'Thank you, sir.'

'A most important study . . . Good morning.'

Out in the corridor and considerably less cheerful than he had been on the previous occasion, Campbell wondered what, apart from informing Jean of this setback, he ought to do next. On the way back over to the unit it occurred to him that in these more desperate circumstances Creech might be worth talking to, if only to find out how the committee had come to the decision Dickie Dunn was now so crisply defending.

In the hope of putting up a better case than he had managed with Dickie Dunn, Campbell went through the problem again. It wasn't that Mkenzi was showering Jean with pot plants and derivative verse: that had done no harm and might even, in a roundabout way, be providing a little cover for Campbell's own more substantial actitivities in the field. Nor was it that he was probably having an affair with the person from nursing: even if he were, it counted as nothing more than a harmless addition to the sum of human happiness.

The problem was simply that he was boring: not a sin or a crime, but an irremediable disability in relation to the study as proposed. To explain that to Creech, no mean bore himself on occasions, might be tricky but worth trying. And if Creech were to be persuaded, perhaps a word from him to Dickie Dunn would eventually result in some reappraisal of the staffing needs of the study before things went off in writing to the trust.

Mkenzi would survive, perhaps going back to Keele with alarming tales of civil rights and colour prejudice in the far North, perhaps eventually more appreciative even of such freedom as he had had to bore people at home in Malawi, and Miss Affleck, her mind enriched and her liberal credentials validated for life by her experience, would find herself a nice local lab technician, settle down and escape forever from the ward-level situation and the added burden of thinking about it.

Creech's secretary was sitting reading a newspaper spread out over her typewriter when Campbell went to make an appointment to see his former chief.

118

'I'm sorry, Dr Campbell, Dr Creech went off to Geneva for ten days this morning. It wasn't anything urgent, was it?'

That afternoon, before Campbell had found an opportunity to ring Jean, she rang him.

'It's mainly about Jim, David. The consultant, Dr Burton, saw him this morning and looked at all the results from the silly tests and had a long talk with him . . .'

'So what's happening?'

'They're letting him out this afternoon . . . I thought they were never going to. But he's to stay at home and they've told him not to work for a while.'

'How are the headaches?'

'That's the worrying bit, David, he's really still having them. Not as bad but oftener, and they really don't go away in between, they just get a bit less.'

'Have they got him on anything for pain?'

'Well, they didn't until yesterday, because of all this nonsense about wanting to see him with a proper headache. But yes. Distalgesic. And it's not doing much good.'

'How is he generally?'

'He's sort of pretending he's better than he is, because he wants out. But he still looks a bit horrible. Pale and ill.'

'Have they told him what they think it is?'

'Well, that's one of the things I wanted to talk to you about. What's this chap Burton like?'

'Sort of old-fashioned and sensible.'

'But honest?'

'What do you mean?'

'Well, does he tell people the truth?'

'Patients?'

'Yes. And relatives.'

'I don't know him terribly well, but he's very straighforward. Not the brightest . . .' Campbell recalled Bill Dempster's remark that Burton wasn't the sort of consultant he'd take a headache of his own to.

'I know that. I just meant does he give you the bad news if it is? Because after he'd talked to Jim and then to me we compared notes and Jim said if that had been Tommy somebody, a consultant we both know in Aberdeen, he'd think he was booked.'

'What do you mean?'

'Well, that Burton chap said we're really not exactly sure about

119

the diagnosis, so we can't say exactly what's going to happen, but you've to go out and enjoy yourself, and keep in touch, as the headaches may go on for a bit longer.'

'Does he know you're both doctors?'

'He knows Jim is. Not sure about me.'

'If he said that to Jim and he knows Jim's a doctor then I would have thought he meant just that.'

'Not that he knows something he thinks we ought not to know?'

'Shouldn't have thought so. Think how often we really don't know what's wrong with people.'

'Thanks, David. Yes. That's sensible. Thanks.'

'He didn't go into possibilities?'

'Not really. He said to Jim, "You're a doctor and you know the sort of things we'd be thinking of." I suppose that means the nasties. Then he said, "There's nothing to confirm your worst suspicions, I'm happy to be able to tell you", then the bit about not knowing and so not being able to say what'll happen. So I'm a bit scared, but not as scared as I'd be if he'd come straight out and said sorry, it's like this, and we know, and this is me telling you.'

'So really he's telling you that there's nothing definite or awful.'

'I suppose so. Thanks, David.'

At this stage in a typical recent phone call between Campbell and Jean, one of them would have said come round soon or can I come round first thing in the morning or how about lunch or I'll cook for us or simply I'm on my way. With Jim due home in a few hours it was less straightforward. There was a long pause.

'David . . .'

'What?'

'Can we meet for lunch tomorrow?'

'Yes please. Shall I come over to Endocrinology?'

'Your flat might be quieter.'

'An odd story. Not really typical of anything. And you can just imagine how old Monty would play it. "Yes, the poor chap with headaches. And you've done one or two of these tests of yours and not found out what's doing it . . . Well, let's wait and see and if it's something serious we'll know soon enough and if it isn't we'll have saved ourselves a lot of trouble . . . But try and get a post-mortem anyway . . . Good morning to you. I'll be down at the college for the rest of the week." What age did you say this chap was?'

'Twenty-six. Maybe twenty-seven.'

'And a bit of weight loss?'

'A little.'

'And definitely no visual symptoms.'

'Pretty sure.'

'And the headache's poorly localised.'

'All over. And worse sometimes than others, but over the last week or so never completely absent.'

'Sounds grim, but something localising would help a lot. Speech all right?'

On the one occasion when Campbell had heard the patient speak he had got through his telephone number without difficulty. 'I think so.'

Hadden frowned. 'Old Monty must have let them do *some* investigations.'

'Skull X-ray, LP, lots of bloods and a carotid angiogram. All negative.'

'That rules out a lot of things.'

'Sorry. The protein was a little bit up.'

'God spare us from minimal abnormalities.'

'Actually it was just the upper limit of normal. And they repeated it, and it was the same. They thought he'd had a fit but he probably hadn't.'

'So they didn't even get the story right?'

'He fell but didn't fit.'

Hadden emptied his glass. 'Hate to find myself agreeing with Monty Burton, but it's probably quite reasonable to wait and see. The chap's not going anywhere, and there are not an awful lot of treatable things that can't wait until the patient helps you a bit more than this chap seems to have done. And if it's a nasty, he'll get localising signs, or start fitting or something, and what's the point of telling the chap, look, we think you're booked but we're not sure? I suppose they could ram some air into his CSF and get slightly better pictures. Maybe. But a pneumo-encephalogram hurts like hell. You can see why Monty's holding off.'

'He doesn't seem to have mentioned that.'

'Of course if this was Boston or the Queen Square Hospital for Funny Walks in London we'd do a CAT scan. But it's not, and we're not going to get one here in time to help your friend.'

'A what?'

'Another great British invention we can't afford. Soft X-rays, scrambled by computer, unscrambled by astrology, I believe. Lovely pictures of your brain, once we get one. Just what this chap needs but there we are. A friend of yours?'

'Sort of. A friend of a friend.'

Bertie MacElwee proved easier to find than Campbell had anticipated. According to Hadden he spent about an hour after lunch most days in a quiet office near the female ward of his general surgical unit 'keeping up with the journals, would you believe, but don't knock if you hear him snoring'.

Campbell listened carefully and then knocked. A quarterdeck bass shouted, 'Come in!' Bertie, in his shirtsleeves and wearing a bow tie even louder than the one on the day of the interview, sprawled in a chair. There was a tidy heap of journals on the floor to the left of him, and little sheaf of torn-out pages in front, and a wild scattering of presumably discarded remnants on the right.

'Yes, boy?'

'Mr MacElwee, I'm sorry to bother you, but you might remember that we met at an appointment committee a couple of weeks ago.'

'Yes. I interviewed you.'

'Well, it's about the study . . . The thing the candidates were being appointed for.'

'Yes, yes.'

'I may be talking out of turn, but I thought it might be worth mentioning to you, as someone who was on the appointment committee, that . . .'

'Come to the point, boy.'

'I know that strictly speaking it was an open interview . . . Applications had been invited, and all that . . . But the way things have worked out . . . well, I thought perhaps it would be worth mentioning that one or two problems have arisen. And as one of the Institute's members of the committee you might like to know how things are going.'

'Just tell me the problem, boy . . .' He paused and squinted thoughtfully at Campbell. 'That chap from Nyasaland turn out to be a cannibal or something?'

'It's not quite as bad as that . . .'

At the end of Campbell's account of the difficulties recently arising Bertie looked thoughtful again then said, 'Not surprised. Guessed as much myself at the time. Trouble with these damned committees is they don't listen to you. Told 'em straight. I've worked out there and I know Johnny Native. Appoint this chap and you'll have no end of trouble. I might as well have saved my breath. You saw 'em yourself. Creech, two vicars and that damned woman who wants nurses to have opinions. All I can say is I did my best, they didn't listen to me and I'm not in the least surprised by what you say.'

'As you probably know, Professor Dunn's been out of the country for a while.'

Bertie snorted gleefully. 'Dickie? Never in it.'

For the next bit Campbell weighed his words carefully. 'He would have been on the committee, I suppose, in the normal course of events. For the Institute . . . So the chap who actually . . .'

'The young vicar . . . Whatsisname?'

'Gordon. Andrew Gordon.'

'Chaplain here . . .'

'Well, assistant chaplain. At the Institute. He might have had a better chance. And he'd thought the whole thing up.'

Bertie narrowed his eyes. 'Really? That bloody vicar never said so, you know. All the more damned fool them for ignoring my advice.'

'That's very interesting, sir . . . I'm not at all sure that Professor Dunn will know any of that.'

'Then I'll bloody well tell him, as soon as he comes back.'

'It's probably more of an Institute matter than the composition of the committee allowed, so I hope you don't mind my raising the matter with you, sir . . . Professor Dunn may actually be back already.'

'I'll give him a ring. Thanks for putting me in the picture, lad, but you're only confirming what was perfectly obvious to me at the interview. I take it you don't mind my passing on what you've just told me?'

'No, sir.'

'Spotted most of it from the look of him . . . Creech and those bloody vicars didn't, you know. Leave it with me, lad . . .'

With that Campbell felt he had done his best, and all he could do now was to await results. As requested, Mkenzi sent an awesome bundle of drafts of his various position papers, which lay on Campbell's desk to the right of the blotting pad, in the space formerly occupied by reprints about faecal vitamins and reserved for things he didn't expect to get round to reading.

Jean's Jim was discharged from hospital and was reported to be lounging around at home, unwell and complaining from time to time of a headache. Over the next week or so his condition changed little. He remained off work and the analgesics prescribed did not seem to help his pain very much. Jean, who was still dropping in at Campbell's flat fairly regularly on her way to work in the morning, continued to worry about him.

One evening she rang Campbell from a payphone in the Casualty Department of the Institute to say that she wanted to come round to see him right away. 'It's all a bit difficult, David, and I really want to talk to you. A couple of things, really. Jim had a fit, a full-blown grand mal seizure about half an hour ago, and they're taking him into ward sixteen again. And there's something else. I think I'm pregnant.'

IV

'So what exactly's wrong with Jean's husband?'

'I don't think anybody really knows.'

'You mentioned he'd been ill but it didn't register that he was actually all that ill, then a couple of days ago I saw his name in one of those lists they send us so I looked in to sixteen to say hello . . . I must say I was a bit surprised.'

'I didn't realise you knew him.'

'Only vaguely,' said Andrew. 'But you must know him.'

'I don't think I've ever met him.'

'Quiet chap, quite bright . . . Perhaps the boring side of serious but they've always seemed very happy together . . . But last week he looked really ghastly. Making the effort to talk, but it did look like an effort. Then I ran into Anna rushing around the Institute with her clipboard and got the most alarming tale, all about fits and cerebral tumours. So I wondered if there was anything definite . . .'

'Not so far as I know.'

'Anna said Jean was being marvellously brave and sensible . . .'

'Yes . . . But I think she's quite worried about him.'

'So Anna said. There seems to be nothing they can do for him, was how she put it.'

Campbell hesitated between allowing Anna's version to stand and appearing too much of an expert on the details of an illness affecting someone he didn't know. 'He's had a lot of headaches and one fit, but as far as I know nobody's very sure what's causing it. I've heard the odd thing about it around the Unit, but there's nothing very definite yet, I gather.'

'Well, that's probably all there is to it . . . I'm always amazed how much doctors know about each others' diseases . . . In fact I once sat through a dinner with an old boy, a retired surgeon, who rattled on about everyone's ghastly problems then admitted over the port that after forty years in medicine hearing about your colleagues' mortal illnesses was by far life's keenest pleasure. Mind you, he was probably drunk.'

Campbell and the assistant chaplain were having one of their

125

periodic lunches in the club. There was no fixed agenda, but a number of topics seemed to both to merit discussion. By the time they retreated to coffee in the lounge only the matter of the ethics study remained.

'Andrew, I had a brief chat with Dickie Dunn about things. . . . It really wasn't terribly encouraging.'

The assistant chaplain smiled. 'I think I mentioned I'd written to him. Got a typical Dickie note by return. Jolly good show, thanks awfully and a terribly important study. Hard lines, of course, but there we are.'

'And after that I went up to see MacElwee. He was even odder than he was at the interview. Asked me if Mkenzi had turned out to be a cannibal.'

'And what did you say . . .? No, really, one shouldn't pry. But he'd know from his Haldane that eating people is wrong.'

Campbell was surprised. 'How did you know about Haldane?'

'Anna again. Really rather a strange girl. Kept telling me she must dash but stood chattering away for about half an hour. In fact quite a lot of it about James, as she calls him. Seemed rather smitten.'

'Could be,' said Campbell, sufficiently vaguely to protect his sources. 'I think she actually enjoys all those position papers and memos to his research staff, as he calls them.'

'Really? That sounds a bit heavy.'

'It is. And then I tried to get hold of Creech, but he's in Geneva. Back in about a week.'

'It's all very interesting,' said Andrew as they left the club. 'One shouldn't be interested, of course, but knowing all the people . . . And Jean's really all right?'

'Seems to be,' said Campbell. 'At least so far.'

'Where am I?' said the man. His eyes opened. 'Am I dead now?'

'No,' said the nurse rather sharply. 'You're in the Institute. Intensive Care. You've had a coronary but you're comfortable.'

'Thank you . . . And does my wife know?'

'She'll be informed shortly by telephone. Just to try to lie quietly, Mr . . . Mr?'

'You're very kind . . . Mr Dunlop, actually, if it's any help.'

'Just try to lie quietly, Mr Dunlop.'

'. . . chest's a bit sore.'

'It's all right. You've had something for the pain.'

'You're very kind . . . Very kind indeed.'

Mr Dunlop smiled and closed his eyes again. He was one of only three or four people Campbell had seen in his entire career who had regained consciousness after cardio-pulmonary resuscitation. He had been admitted to Intensive Care twenty minutes previously, having collapsed at a Rotary dinner. Grey and shocked, he had mumbled his answers to Campbell's routine questions, drifting in and out of a not unpleasant confusional state in which he alternately declined and accepted a variety of drinks with great politeness.

His cardiac arrest had gone just as the books directed. Suddenly pale, pulseless and unconscious, with Campbell and a nurse already at his bedside and the duty anaesthetist quite fortuitously also around, he had taken the endotracheal tube first shot and constricted his pupils again almost as soon as the external cardiac massage had been started. Now he was back in sinus rhythm and conscious once more.

'You're very kind, all of you.'

'What age is he?'

'Sixty-four.'

'Looks older. First coronary?'

'Yes, thank you.'

'Anyone with him?'

'Yes, but he's drunk as well.'

'Very kind, all of you.'

'Just try to lie quietly, Mr Dunlop.'

The anaesthetist was grinning alternately at the monitor and the staff nurse, who was tidying away the various ampoules, syringes and items of packaging that accumulated at the scene of any resuscitation attempt. Campbell, more familiar with what had to be done when the patient stayed dead than with what was needed now, hung about in the cubicle, aware that he would require eventually to complete his systematic enquiry but not in any hurry to do so.

The nurse spotted him and presented him with a handful of empty ampoules. He was about to throw them in the appropriate receptacle when she stopped him. 'You're supposed to write up everything we've given him. In the drug Kardex. It's over there, doctor.'

'Thank you, staff nurse.'

'Everyone's so kind here.'

'Hello? David? Is it a bad time to phone?'

'No. It's just gone quiet.'

'Have you been busy?'

127

There was another little burst of activity around eight o'clock, mainly people with things they didn't want to bother a doctor with in the middle of the night. Campbell's intention to ring Jean at home to discuss breakfast before he left the department was lost in a flurry of last-minute X-rays to exclude unlikely fractures.

He rang her as soon as he got back to his flat. There was no reply. He went back to the door for the papers and the mail, which included a handwritten note from Dickie Dunn requesting his attendance at a 'brief informal meeting to discuss the ethics study', to take place in his office at three that afternoon.

After breakfast and a shower, he rang the Institute and asked for Jean's extension. It was answered by the Endocrinology Outpatients receptionist, who said that Dr Moray wasn't in yet, and asked if that was Dr Campbell calling again and could she take a message. Unable to think of any message which could in the circumstances be left with a receptionist, he said it wasn't urgent and went to bed, setting his alarm clock for half past one.

'I can't imagine what all this is about. James certainly doesn't need any help from a lot of people who don't know anything about moral philosophy. Do you know, David?'

'No idea. I just got the note about it this morning.'

Anna Affleck, once more wearing her pink paramilitary outfit, seemed for some reason gratified by that. 'I got mine yesterday . . . And how are you, David? It's ages since we've seen you.'

'All right.'

'Work going well?'

'Yes, thanks. And you?'

'Well, the study's taking up more and more of my time, but I'm still able to fit everything in. And Brenda doesn't mind. I'd really done most of the work for my MSc before all this started, and she's terribly keen on it. The study, I mean. And of course she gets on like a house on fire with James. Makes jokes about us colonials sorting out the old country.'

'So that's what they're doing.'

'Sarcasm doesn't become you, David . . . James may have his faults but he's just the chap to take on a thing like this in Edinburgh. He knows a terrific amount about British tradition and thought, from his PhD work, and yet he's from completely outside the tradition. It wouldn't occur to these people . . .' She tossed her head scathingly in the direction of Dickie Dunn's desk, '. . . . to attack the problem at its roots by meshing a good-going philosophical

157

input into the medical curriculum as a whole, rather than just dithering round the edges as some other people might have done.'

'I'm not sure the study . . .'

'I know,' snapped Anna, in a way that reminded Campbell of her mentor. 'But that doesn't stop someone like James from going to the heart of the problem.'

Anna had arrived first for Professor Dunn's meeting, Campbell, at a few minutes to three, second. There seemed to be more chairs in the office than on the former occasion: six, in addition to the old-fashioned wooden swivel chair behind the desk, were arranged in a rough semi-circle in front of it. Campbell did a little juggling of names and numbers, then noticed a side table with tea things — seven cups and saucers — in the corner furthest from the window.

At exactly three o'clock Jean came in, followed by Andrew. She looked relaxed and happy, and smiled first at Anna then, as though she had just noticed him and was pleased to see him, at Campbell. Anna looked from her watch to the door and then again at her watch.

At one minute past, Dickie Dunn came in, followed by his secretary, who was carrying a large, rather elegant teapot. He looked quickly round the group as though checking it against a list then turned to his secretary. 'Pour for five, please, Miss Nisbet.'

Campbell and Andrew exchanged glances, Andrew nodding slightly. Jean, who was standing on Anna's left, winked at Campbell with her left eye. Anna looked anxiously round towards the door.

'Please sit down, everyone.' Professor Dunn took a plate of plain biscuits from the side table and started to go round. 'Andrew . . ? Campbell? Good of you to come. And you must be Dr Moray . . . I was sorry to hear your husband's been a little under the weather.'

Jean smiled again. 'He's actually very much better now, thank you.'

'Delighted to hear that . . . Anna? A biscuit? Sorry about these, but the University Grants Committee insists we economise . . .'

With the tea ceremony well under way, the secretary retreated and Dickie, instead of taking his place behind the desk, sat down next to Andrew and smiled around for order.

'I think I've indicated to most of you that this would be a short and informal meeting . . . It might now turn out to be very short indeed.' Jean smiled at Campbell and Anna gripped her nasty little shiny handbag as though it had fought loose from her on several occasions since she had entered the room.

'We have one apology and one . . .' He paused to weigh his

words. 'It would be imprecise to call it a resignation. Perhaps a withdrawal. Professor Hamilton sends his apologies, and I understand that he is reconsidering his position as a grant-holder. Dr Mkenzi . . .' All except Professor Dunn glanced more or less openly in the direction of Anna Affleck, '. . . has withdrawn his application. For family reasons, as I understand it.'

Unnoticed or perhaps ignored by Professor Dunn, Anna sniffed. 'I took it upon myself,' he continued, 'as perhaps sole grant-holder, to drop him a note expressing gratitude for his interest in the study, nothing more. And I'm sure we all wish him well. Andrew, I believe, is ready to assume the major responsibility for this most important piece of work, and I firmly believe the rest of you will help him a very great deal. Unless someone else has some other urgent matter to raise I think that more or less concludes our business, so if any of you have to slip away . . . However, there are a few more of these wholesome UGC biscuits . . .'

Anna chose to slip away very quickly indeed. Professor Dunn rose as she left, and Andrew and Campbell followed suit. To Campbell's surprise, Jean followed swiftly after, not saying goodbye, but simply smiling and nodding towards Professor Dunn as she left. The ladies having withdrawn, Dunn allowed himself a wheezy chuckle, and clearly had something to confide to Andrew and Campbell. He sipped his tea and twinkled. 'Family reasons is putting it fairly mildly.'

'Nothing serious, I hope,' said Andrew.

'Depends on your view of these things . . . It occurred to me the blighter might be over here with some sort of official support, and might perhaps not be in a position to offer us his services, splendid though they may be, without at least seeking official permission. So I rang up the Malawian High Commission in London, and got the most amiable of cultural attachés, who was extremely interested in the whereabouts of our friend.'

Dunn paused and twinkled again. 'Not just what I thought he was up to . . . Jumping bail on his government-sponsored post-doctoral fellowship. A bit more to it than that. That's where the family reasons come in. A Mrs Mkenzi and about seven — I suppose one should call them wee — Mkenzis had turned up at Keele looking for our moral philospher, and failing to find him had naturally got in touch with the High Commission. So it's next plane home, I should have thought. And isn't Malawi the place that's run by that octogenarian Presbyterian Sunday-school teacher chappie?'

On the way downstairs Andrew seemed pleased rather than elated. 'Most interesting,' he said. 'The whole thing might be rather fun now. And wasn't that good news about Jean's husband?'

'Yes,' said Campbell. 'Did she say what they'd found?'

'Didn't have a chance to ask. Only just met her on the way in. . . I really must try to pop over to the Southern and see him . . .'

They had coffee on the lawn and discussed possible names for the multi-disciplinary discussion groups that would once more constitute the basic means of enquiry into what Andrew called 'a couple of topics that seem to bother people', until it was time for him to go down to Calvin College for a four o'clock tutorial.

Though Campbell was tired, there didn't seem much point in trying to get any sleep before going on duty at six, and though he would have liked to talk to Jean, he had gained the impression that any attempt to contact her that afternoon might be unsuccessful. In the event he went back over to Rosamund's unit, to check in the secretary's room whether there was any mail for him that had not been forwarded to Casualty. There was none. On the way out he met Creech, and realised that he had probably erred in not seeking a now-lettest-thou-thy-servant-depart-in-peace interview with him before leaving for his new job.

'Don't apologise. I'm away so much these days that that happens all the time. And I only got back from Geneva a few days ago. How are you enjoying Surgical Outpatients?'

'Quite different from what I was doing, sir, and very interesting.'

'Glad to hear it . . . And how about that other thing you were involved in . . ? Something to do with ethics, wasn't it?'

'Yessir. That seems to be getting under way again.'

'Again?'

'There was a mix up about an appointment, but it seems to have been sorted out now.'

'Now that was the thing with the ministers, wasn't it?'

'Yessir.'

'A very odd wee committee. What's happened now? That chap from Malawi no good?'

'It seems to have been sorted out now, sir. He's withdrawn and the other chap's doing it.'

'Well, they can't say I didn't warn them. But that woman, Bobby MacElwee and . . . Aithie. Yes, Aithie. They just wouldn't listen.'

'Really, sir?'

'MacElwee was quite extraordinary. Never seen anything like it in about thirty years of these committees. Said he knew all about those chaps, and we couldn't go wrong with somebody from whatever tribe he thought he was from. I'm not even sure he got the tribe right, but I'm glad to hear it's all water under the bridge now . . . So the local chap got it after all? I'm sure Professor Hamilton will be very pleased about that, because for someone who was supposed to be in the chair he really backed the local chap quite strongly. But Bobby kept saying, listen to me, I *know* these chaps.'

'Really?'

'So you're getting on with it now?'

'Yessir.'

'Well, best of luck. And as I said, if I can help you with a reference or a word somewhere, don't hesitate to ask.'

Campbell went back to his flat for another shower, as a poor substitute for inadequate sleep. Behind the door he found a note from Jean, on a five by eight index card headed 'Royal Charitable Institute — Endocrinology Outpatients'. There was no Dear David. It read, 'Jim had the pneumo thing yesterday and it helped a lot, because he had an operation this morning to remove a colloid cyst of third ventricle (I think), which means he's cured. Thanks for being so marvellous. I'll ring you tonight. XX Jean.'

At six Campbell was back in Casualty. It was quiet, and Hadden was in the back room relaxing over a coffee. 'Cheer up, lad. Tonight shouldn't be so dull. And think how much more you know about everything than you did last night.'

'Thanks.'

'J G mentioned that he'd had a look through some of your notes, and he's not too worried about you.'

'So big brother watches you?'

'God, wouldn't you, if you were in charge of this place, with two or three hundred potential lawsuits walking in and out every day? And he means it quite nicely.'

'I suppose so.' As Campbell was putting on his white coat it occurred to him that Hadden might be interested in the outcome of the case they had discussed a couple of times already. 'Graham, remember that chap I mentioned. Sore head, falls and a couple of fits. He turned out to have . . .'

Hadden snapped his fingers quite vehemently. 'I'll tell you what he had. A paraphyseal cyst of third ventricle.'

'Nearly,' said Campbell, nonetheless impressed. 'A colloid cyst of third ventricle.'

'It's the same thing, you ignorant bugger.'

'Oh. How did you know it was that?'

'Because that's what it sounded like once I'd thought about it. Intermittent symptoms and practically nothing on the standard investigations. They get written off as hysterics first and brain tumours later, so the well-educated neurologist can usually get it over the phone. And they do very well when it's tweaked out. He'll be fine.'

'So I gather. What is it?'

'A wee cyst, benign, that sits in the third ventricle and obstructs CSF circulation. So they get intermittent acute hydrocephalus. Pretty obvious once I'd thought about it. I shouldn't think Monty Burton's ever heard of it, but it's probably in that wee book of yours, under H for headache.'

Jean did not ring that night, or if she did Campbell was too immersed in the avalanche of miscellaneous emergencies, great and small, to be called to the phone. It lasted from half past eight until around five o'clock, when it slowed to a pace comparable to Thursday night at its worst. Hadden stayed till four, and when Campbell got off duty he went home and slept from nine thirty to half past five, when it was time to get up and go back to work again.

For the rest of his week on nights he heard nothing from Jean. Towards the end of it he heard from Andrew, who rang him at home full of good news about the study. Details of the appointments had now gone to the trust, which had responded by expressing renewed enthusiasm based partly, it appeared, on reports from Dr Arnold. The original level of support had been extended to two years, and an offer of increased support if any new topic which merited study was being discussed by the grant-holders. (It transpired that Professor Hamilton had had occasion to further reconsider his position, and was now restored.)

However, the main point of the phone call, Andrew stressed, was to invite Campbell to a little dinner at the club, for six only and intended as a small celebration of the rescue and re-launch of the Multi-disciplinary Health Care Ethics Study.

For a variety of reasons, Campbell accepted. The dinner took place the following week, by which time the world was right way up again, and daytime casualty work simply a pleasant and stimulating alternative to previous employment. Campbell arrived early, hoping perhaps to have a word with Jean over the sherry, but she arrived late, and sat between Professor Dunn and

Professor Hamilton, as inaccessible to Campbell, sitting beyond Anna on the other side of the table, as she had been for the previous ten days.

There was a fair amount to drink, and everyone except Campbell and Anna talked a lot. The senior men traded anecdotes, Dickie's being by far the better, and Jean, happy and bright-eyed, chattered contentedly about her husband's near-miraculous deliverance. Only as they were moving through for coffee did she and Campbell speak, and then only briefly. She asked him if he took sugar, which was a private joke from more than a year ago, then said, 'How are you, David?'

'All right.'

'You always say that.'

'How are you?'

'We're fine.' She leaned closer, reaching for the cream jug. 'And I'm not even . . .' She lowered her voice, '. . . pregnant any more.'

Campbell was shocked and it showed. Jean shook her head emphatically. 'Gosh no. I wouldn't have done that. More a case of I probably wasn't at all in the first place . . . Stress, I suppose. One lump or two, Dr Campbell?'

On the steps outside afterwards, the party broke up slowly. Campbell had left his car at home because Jean, usually a very moderate drinker, would almost certainly be taking hers and the offer of a lift home would have been perhaps the minimum gesture to be expected after all that had happened.

As things turned out Andrew took care of Professor Dunn, and Jean of Professor Hamilton. As they walked off to their respective cars Campbell found Anna, unpleasantly drunk for a woman but perhaps understandably so, standing close to his elbow jingling her car keys in her hand. 'I have my car with me, David, if you'd like a lift to Marchmont.'

The planning stage of the revived study took longer than expected, with Andrew and one or other of the research associates going round and explaining the nature of the exercise to a wide variety of doctors, nurses and university people. With Campbell back on nights again and Jean on holiday with her convalescent husband, Anna did more than her share and turned out, according to Andrew, to be quite good under the right sort of supervision.

The next occasion on which they all gathered together was rather an unexpected one, a memorial service for Professor Hamilton, who had died suddenly not long after his rehabilitation, collapsing in the courtyard of Calvin College, at the feet of the statue of John Knox.

The service took place in the university church, and was well attended by both churchmen and academics. Campbell went along on his own, seeing Anna before she saw him in the crowd going in and managing to avoid her. Proceeding up the opposite aisle, he was directed by an usher into a pew in which, to his mild astonishment, Jean was already sitting.

She smiled at him as he joined her. The pew filled up and eventually they were compelled to sit very close together. They shared a hymn book and sat listening to a eulogy by Professor Aithie, who stressed the deceased's great range of interests, citing his key role in the development of a multi-disciplinary study of ethics as only the most recent example of many such initiatives.

They left together and, in the discreetly sociable crowd around the church door, neither seemed in any particular hurry to leave the other. They remained together, chatting vaguely about Professor Hamilton with rather more eye contact than was usual in the circumstances, while lots of people they both vaguely knew dispersed across the grass and gravel of the churchyard.

A sudden, brief peal of laughter made them both look round. To Campbell's surprise it appeared to have come from Andrew, who was standing in conversation with Dickie Dunn and was already looking slightly embarrassed. Seeing Campbell, Dickie raised a hand to catch his attention, then both he and Andrew came across.

'Glad I've caught you two,' said Dickie. 'About the ethics study. It's all off.'

'Off?' said Campbell and Jean together.

'Yes. Off. I could have let people know a couple of days ago but . . .' He nodded back at the church. 'Didn't want to spoil old Hammy's party.'

'What's happened?'

'The money's funny,' said Dickie. Andrew laughed again, more quietly this time. 'Had a couple of phone calls from the university accountant,' Dickie continued, 'asking what the hell's going on. Dollars flying through your account in thousands, from these Sanford people and off all over Europe, on their signature. He thought Yugoslavia was suspicious but really put his foot down about Albania, even if it *was* for student groups studying medical ethics.'

Campbell remembered his visit from Dr Arnold while he was on duty in ICU, and nodded. Jean looked puzzled. Andrew explained.

'In this job we sometimes have to baptise money, so to speak, but we're supposed to draw the line at laundering it. Even in the defence of western civilisation.' Jean nodded too.

Dickie and Andrew, still laughing, went off in search of Anna. Jean and Campbell walked back in the general direction of the Institute, taking, since the afternoon was pleasant, a little detour through the park. When they reached the side gate of the hospital they stopped, both facing half towards Marchmont.

Jean spoke first. 'It's funny. Services like that never take as long as you expect. I'd arranged to take the whole afternoon off.'

'So had I.'

'And we haven't seen each other properly for ages.'